Robert Somers

**The Martyr of Glencree**

Vol. 2

Robert Somers

**The Martyr of Glencree**
*Vol. 2*

ISBN/EAN: 9783337347208

Printed in Europe, USA, Canada, Australia, Japan

Cover: Foto ©Andreas Hilbeck / pixelio.de

More available books at **www.hansebooks.com**

# THE MARTYR OF GLENCREE.

## *A ROMANCE TOO TRUE.*

By ROBERT SOMERS.

IN THREE VOLUMES.

VOL. II.

London :

SAMPSON LOW, MARSTON, SEARLE, & RIVINGTON,

CROWN BUILDINGS, 188, FLEET STREET.

1878.

# THE MARTYR OF GLENCREE.

## CHAPTER I.

The seeds of ill, the dormant lust, the prompt
Advice of old conceits or new intents
Of love or malice, and all the web-like
Roots of wayward sin and selfness, are strewn
So thickly in our core, and find so quick
And sharp a soil, it hath been known full oft
That accidents of rain, sun, touch of frost,
Or hap of snow, have given them life and spring,
And push'd them into rank luxuriance.

*Anon.*

PICARDY, on passing out of the ravine, which,
as seemed to him, had been nearly fatal to
his life, soon lost the elation of spirit in
which he had found himself again in free
possession of his drove. He sang no more
jolly songs that evening, or songs of any

kind, but fell into as deep reveries as a
mind like his could pursue.  Yet his studies,
brown as they were, seemed to spur him by
rapidly-recurring starts on the road, and the
Arab was kept in lively motion from the
right hand to the left speeding forward the
weary cattle.

It had been the intention of the drover
to rest his beasts on Glenvernoch that
evening.  He might find the farmer more
disposed to deal; he would have an opportunity of seeing and knowing more of what
was going on " about the toon," for Picardy,
almost unconsciously to himself, had taken
on to his profession of cattle-buyer the
function of a spy, and if he should carry
down both beasts and information from
Glenvernoch along with him to Wigtown
he had joy of thinking what advantage he
would have over the too authoritative and
mpatient tactics of his officious friend the

Bailie. The little magistrate would have to play second fiddle to him after that.

But this view of affairs had been much changed by what had occurred within the last hour. Of information from the upper borders at least of Glenvernoch he had more than he himself could well comprehend or digest. The farm might be a bed of treason, or merely the innocent harbour of a love affair on its outer margin. That Glenvernoch had any act or part in this love affair Picardy could not reconcile with his personal knowledge of the farmer. He had ostensibly owed his life to the sudden appearance of the women on the scene, and to Margaret in particular, who seemed to be more offended at Hay than at himself. That Glenvernoch would be more disposed to part with his three-year-olds on low terms by any version he could give of his encounter with Hay, was as improbable as that he could venture either on much mendacity or much cajolery in presence of Glenvernoch's daughter. The more Picardy conned the situation the more he felt that in Glenvernoch that night he would be in little better case than a hedgehog, forced to roll himself into the smallest compass, finding neither sympathy nor point of attack on one side or the other. So he gave a wide berth to the farm-house, and resolved to push on to the valley of the Bladnoch, within two or three miles of the county town, and discharge himself of the weighty enough business he had already in hand.

What ghosts of more secret, and sweet though guilty thought flitted through the brain of the drover, as he began once more, in his free and easy spirit, to think that all was going right, could be known only to himself, and by himself only half known at the best. Tam had a rough, native, abiding sort of attachment to the old families and substantial farmers of the shire. He had lived and made money among them since he began to be the man he was. No one of the common rank had seen more of the gentle life of Galloway or been more deeply touched by unavailing fancies, secret fannings of what might be love, or impossible ambitions. Nowhere had he been more at home in his calling than at Baldoon. He had observed Martha since she was a playful girl hanging on the arm of her father while going about the parks looking at the stock, and chaffering or arranging with the dealer ; had seen her growing into womanhood, received her smile, and heard her merry laugh in the hall ; had looked at her as one might look at a sweet, full, foreign flower through the panes of a conservatory, and would like to pluck it, but could not. And so this ad-

miration of Picardy remained a fancy and
no more, among many other fancies of a
like kind which rose in his open heart as
he passed from the castles to the farm-
houses, and saw in both many fair women
of his own rank not unworthy to be his
bride.    To say that he had ever made love
to Margaret would not be exact, for freely
as he bandied love phrases about, he had
never ventured so far with the daughter of
Glenvernoch, any more than he could
hitherto have ventured such familiarity
with the gentle daughter of the Baron of
Baldoon.    The youth, intelligence, up-
rightness of character, and graceful manner of Margaret had exercised a fascina-
tion over Picardy, which stood in his books
like a large balance of account in her favour;
and there the matter rested.    But his
fancy, in its freer and wilder moods, returned more frequently to Martha than to

others; and in times of civil disorder strange psychological disorders affect the minds of many common enough kind of people.

Picardy well knew of the early attachment of Martha to William Hay of Arioland. But Hay had been for some years a lost man to all who were of Picardy's way of thinking—one whom anybody could shoot down on meeting him, and have State reward and favour for so loyal a deed. Yet, though Picardy's moral sense had freely traversed this wide space of right and wrong, he retained a loyal kind of feeling towards the old families of the province. He had an intuitive, or shrewdly business-like perception, that they would survive the storms of the time. He could never quite agree with the Bailie that they would be blown away at the blast of Clavers, and when the little, fussy magistrate of

Wigtown vowed that the broad lands of the Stewarts, Dalrymples, M'Dowalls, Gordons, and Dunbars would be the possession of the Grahams and the Grahamites, Picardy usually whistled or hummed a tune in a vague way, as if he were thinking of something else. But the native families, and their more thriving tenants, were for the present paralyzed. They had no dealings in cattle or in much else. The Clavers' faction in the province, and those who hung upon its skirts, seeking to make profit out of the hard measures, and to share in the final spoils of the time, were the only parties taking up stock. Why should not he, Picardy, deal with those who for the present were the only active dealers? Why not be friendly and confiding to them in matters a little beyond the actual transactions as he had been in a civil way in other cases? "To make hay while the sun shines " was a proverb of the country which Tam devoutly, though perhaps not quite morally, believed in.

Even if, as he surmised, the native gentry should survive the fines and harryings of the period, and the old authorities be restored, what could be said but that he had been following his usual and lawful profession ? On the other hand, if the Clavers' *régime* should prevail, and much change of property ensue, he might expect to become a man of wealth, honour, and distinction beyond the measure of all the more officious time-servers. He could picture in that event the Laird of Baldoon an impoverished and afflicted old man— Hay shot, banished, executed, or driven a hopeless fugitive to the ends of the world —Martha wandering on the moors needful of protection—and a crisis when the intervention of a rich cattle-dealer, with some

acres of his own, would be an effectual
solvent of all distinctions of rank between
the families of Picardy and Dunbar.

When the drover rode into Wigtown,
next morning, he went direct to the residence of Sheriff-depute Graham. He
had somehow an indelible impression that
it was with the Sheriff-depute he had to
do, though strictly and properly he should
have seen the Bailie. But Picardy had
been struck with the eager demand for
cattle that had sprung up of late in quarters where he had not found it before.
The Sheriff's treasury was overflowing
with funds at this period. Under increased cess, extraordinary levies, and
special fines, the revenues had made such
rapid progress that the Sheriff-clerk could
not overtake the accounts, and a special
officer of finance had been appointed whom
the Sheriff-depute had under his direct

control. A well-defined portion of the total receipts was due to the King's exchequer at Edinburgh, but the accounts became so intricate, what with expenses of collection, charges and discharges, that it was difficult to find out what the net proceeds were; and compositions for fines had often an equivocal destination. Claverhouse, on entering upon possession of his barony of Freuch, found it sadly wasted and eaten up by his own dragoons, and by the surveillance and harassment to which he had subjected, till he finally dispossessed in process of law, its legitimate owner. To re-stock Freuch would be good for the agricultural improvement of the country. Grierson of Lagg, notwithstanding his ardent zeal in the cause of the King and Episcopacy, was also suspected of having a desire to transfer an unlimited quantity of the Galloway cattle to his lands in Dumfriesshire on terms as much as possible under the market value. The Sheriff-depute himself had already gone into some grazing in the vicinity of Wigtown, and was looking forward to being baron, if not of Baldoon, of some other eligible estate. A "cattle ring" had formed itself closely round the Sheriffdom of Galloway, all the links of which Picardy could not pretend to know; but he had a shrewd notion that Sheriff Graham was the key of the work.

The Sheriff-depute heard Picardy's report of his purchases up the Cree with an air of unconcern. So many head of "black nowt," so many "kyloes" heifers, geldings, &c., at such and such prices. "A good marketing," said the Sheriff, "and the Bailie, I have no doubt, will make profit of them to you, Tam."

"And to himsel', Sherra," replied the drover.

"Of course, but that's no concern o' mine—ye're able enough to settle it between ye," remarked the Sheriff, dismissing that part of the subject, and proceeding to put the drover to a searching interrogatory as to what he had seen or heard up the country bearing on public affairs. Picardy was full to the mouth of his meeting with Hay, as in one point of view it seemed to him a stronger quiver to his bow than the drove itself; and yet in another point of view he did not well know how to dissociate the tragic incident, as he deemed it, from some of the circumstances around it. However, after remarking that he had seen or heard little, all was so quiet and usual-like, till within the last twenty-four hours, he went on to narrate the sudden assault of Hay, the attempt of the outlaw to turn back the drove, his own heroic effort to capture Hay, and the encounter that ensued, in which one or other of them would certainly have been killed but for the appearance on the scene of Martha Dunbar and Margaret Wilson of Glenvernoch.

"Was it on the farm of Glenvernoch?" inquired the Sheriff.

"I canna say it was," replied Picardy, and describing the locality, added, "it's on the marches o' Glenvernoch, but they ha'e never been weel rede, I believe, at that point."

"Glenvernoch must be resetting that villain Hay," said the Sheriff, "as well as his mistress Martha of Baldoon. The presence of Martha in company with the farmer's daughter is proof positive of the treacherous and hypocritical connivance of the farmer."

"Weel, to be plain and honest," replied Picardy, "I canna say sae much. The young women, I rather think, had been oot for a walk on a fine afternoon, or to put the worse face on't, maybe Martha had some tryst wi' Hay, and unkent to the ither took her alang wi' her. Margaret was as angry as blazes at Hay, and looked at him as if she had never seen him in the face before. Na, na, depend on't, Hay must hae some wilder howff than Glenvernoch."

"Granting he has," exclaimed the Sheriff, " why should the farmer harbour Martha Dunbar, and so be harbouring Hay? The Bailie has given a bad report of Glenvernoch, and as for his daughter, the Curate says she is the most untractable young woman in the parish. The farmer's conduct, according to the Bailie, was most uncivil and insulting. It's he and Kircailie, and such sneck-drawing farmers—who, because they pay their rents and have some stock and influ-

ence, as they think, even when their lairds
have been snapped off their shoulders, keep
the country in all this disturbance."

"That may be the Bailie's opinion,"
said Picardy, "but I ken the country and
the country-folk better than the Bailie.
Glenvernoch was nae mair unceevil than he
wadna part ceevilly wi' his nowt at what
he thocht less than their value. I hae
seen Glenvernoch in the same fuffle a score
o' times. As for Kircailie, maist o' this
drove are aff his farm. I had nae difficulty
there in making a bargain. What does
the Bailie ken aboot dealing wi' stock
farmers?"

"Your information is very important,
Mr. Picardy," said the Sheriff, after some
silence. "You will see the Bailie, who
talks of nothing else but buying farm
stock, and employing his money in that
direction. You and he, I think, might

extend the line in geldings of good breed profitably. They are in some demand by the Government, and, I hear, are very low in price."

And the drover being about to take his leave, Sheriff-depute Graham, looking among his papers, added, " By the way, Tam, here is a little piece of official business. The sentence passed on the old lady of Arioland has carried forfeiture of her personal property. The officers go down to-morrow to take possession, and if you would go as a judicial valuer, and see that the live stock known to have been about the jointure house is properly surrendered, and no starvelings put in their place, it will be a Government service, and be well paid for."

## CHAPTER II.

I hear a voice you cannot hear,
  Which says I must not stay;
I see a hand you cannot see,
  Which beckons me away.

*Irish Ballad.*

EVENTS follow each other, and the scene shifts from one point to another rapidly at this part of our narrative. We have to look into the farmhouse of Glenvernoch about the same quiet breakfast hour as the interview of Picardy with Sheriff Graham.

Martha and Margaret, on their return from the Crag the previous evening, had arrived just in time to save their credit with the farmer, who, busying about the affairs of "the toon" as usual, had walked out from the steading and looked anxiously up the various paths of the glen more than once.

"They're pretty linties thae," he said to the goodwife, on going into the house. "Pretty linties!"

"Wha are ye speaking aboot, Glen?" said Mrs. Wilson.

"Wha should I be speaking aboot?" quoth Glenvernoch, "but lady Martha and Maggie. Nae sign o' them yet, and noo the darkening."

"Dear me, Glen," replied the wife, "the lasses hae been hame mair than half an hour sine. They're up the stair pitting by their hoods—dae ye want to see them?"

"Na, na, guidwife; if the weans are hame that's a' weel eneuch. I'll see them by and by."

At supper Margaret told her father of

the passing of Picardy's drove, and the respects and promise the drover had asked her to deliver, in case he should not see Glenvernoch himself.

"Ay, ay, Mag, Tam's a cunning chiel," said Glenvernoch. "He likes to reckon when a's by. How mony head were there, do ye ken? Did ye coont them, lady Martha?" asked the farmer, putting question after question without waiting for distinct replies, and becoming so deeply engaged in thoughts of his own as to where the drove might have been lifted, what the prices, and who the real buyers might be, as to exhaust the discourse of the evening.

Martha, who next morning had announced to the farmer and his wife with firmness, but with no little mark of deep eeling, her departure from Glenvernoch on the following day, spent some hours with Margaret in the garret chamber, where, as

to a sister, she opened her heart more
freely. Both had a foreboding that what
had occurred the previous day would be
carried down the country, through Picardy,
reach the ear of the authorities at Wigtown,
and bring a hue and cry on the farm of
Glenvernoch. Margaret, while quivering
under the thought of this probable event,
and more especially the effect it might have
on her father, had nerve enough to look
into the future with bravery and composure.
Martha, while confident in the measures
of Hay for her immediate personal safety,
was more open to the most cruel anguish
of spirit.

It was grief, poignant enough, that in
this wandering exile from Baldoon, originally forced upon her by the stern behest of
the Government, there was no kindness or
hospitality she received, however dear and
sacred, that might not be visited with swift

revenge on her friends by her persecutors.
And if she raised her view a moment from
this unselfish but agonizing consideration
to her own immediate case, to the place
where she was going or the place she might
go to—to the wild retreats of Monygove or
the strong castle and broad fields of Baldoon—there were only clouds of peril and
darkness on either hand—dark, dense, and
blinding.   Martha burst into tears and
sobbings, which seemed to open the foun-
tains of her life, and to rend her heart.

"Oh! mistress Martha," said Margaret,
after unavailing efforts of comfort, "my
dear   Martha—sister—friend—companion
in trouble—be more like yoursel'—do, dear
Martha.   Is there no a God above us, and
a tender, loving Saviour, whose words are
speaking to us noo as they spoke at Be-
thany?   What have we to fear?   What
harm can come to us?   What is the world,

or what may befa' in the world, compared to the crown of glory ?"

" True, true," said Martha, as she looked up to this strong voice out of her distress. "That has been my stay. It is our only stay. Dear Margaret, if there is a saint on earth you must be one. But human feelings are sometimes overpowering. My love for Hay is stronger than life or death; my love for my father is equally unquenchable. These loves are like twin-roots in my heart. They cannot be torn asunder. They must grow together, or they must perish together. My good old father! would like to take me to his arms, yet cannot command me to return, cannot even write me without a warning, as if he feared the result should I be so free. Is it wrong, Margaret, tell me, is it wrong that I should cling to Hay, who is still a free, unstained, and unsubdued soldier of the Covenant? Should I cling to him even in his hour of weakness and despair?"

"Dear Martha," replied Margaret, "ye put a question which could only be answered for ane's sel' in like circumstances. Hoo can I answer for anither in circumstances different? But if I ken my ain weak heart I wouldna put either faither or lover atween me and the love o' Christ, and in ony struggle for the Crown Rights o' the King of kings I would cling to the human strength about me that was truest and nearest to Him."

"O Margaret Wilson!" exclaimed Martha, as she clasped her companion's hands, "how you read my very heart! Yet alas! my heart is wavering like a leaf under momently varying winds. How am I to know where the human strength is to which I should cling, or even the road I should go to-morrow? A breath, a feather, would almost turn me this way or that. If my brother were alive I think I would go to Baldoon, and covering myself under the strength of my father's house, plead on my bended knees for Hay."

"How sae?" inquired Margaret, with a look of timid amazement. "Your brother was—an unhappy man—became a conformer—and had an untimely end. What a story it was!"

"Peace, Marget," said Martha, lowering her voice almost to a whisper. "Ye hae heard o' his bridal as wildly tauld in the country, but ye canna understand it, the grief it brought on us, or the change it wrought on my once happy brother. He turned moody, discontent, restless, without comfort; but he battled with his torn spirit, and buried himself in privacy and in studies, yet was aye gentle as a lamb, and couldna bear the sicht o' pain, or blood, or wrangling. He seemed as years mellowed his sorrow to make a world of his own, in which there would be nothing but peace and calm. And when the change in the Kirk cam' he made nae difference, attended the worship as usual, till there were none but himsel' and the Curate. Mr. Symson was sic a bookman they were aften together. But the Curate was zealous for the new things, perplexed at the desertion o' his service, and angry at the best o' the parishioners who wouldna attend. Strange, he was angriest at Widow Lachlison, a good old soul, whose house is near to the parish kirk, and who is respected by every ane for her management, honesty, and piety. Nane of a' the common folk Sir David liked so well as old Margaret, she was so blameless, had maintained herself so honourably and decently, and was so well informed and read in the Scriptures.

The Curate said to my brother that he believed Mrs. Lachlison was the greatest obstacle to his work in the parish, for, living so near the kirk and yet absenting herself, others on the back-lying farms thocht it their duty to do no otherwise. Her example, were she to comply, would be worth mair than a' the Government edicts. And David often looked in on the widow, finding her with her calm, gentle countenance, and soft, clear eyes, tidily put on, in her clean house, a little round table before her, on which lay the open Bible and the spectacles over the pages where she had been reading. She had had many family afflictions o' her ain, till a' worldly things melted oot o' her heart, leaving only heavenliness. She pitied my brother, and often prayed for him, and gave him such discourse when he went in to talk to her that he came out more affected and edified

in his ain heart by her sayings than any
hope he had of bringing her to the feet of
the Curate.  But as the severities increased,
and scarce any o' the old folk were safe
under their ain roof trees, my brother grew
sick-weary, left Baldoon for Edinburgh,
and fell or was thrown from his horse, when
out riding on the shore at Leith.  He was
taken up dead, Margaret, dead!—my poor,
unhappy brother!"

Martha bent her face, and wept, as she
thus recalled the tragic life and death of
her brother, Margaret observing her in
silent sympathy and respect.

"With a' my mirthfu'ness," continued
the young lady, "I am sure I hae been a
sister of sorrows since I could know what
sorrow was, though only in the bitter tears
and heartbreakings of older people.  The
young, like you and me, Marget, can hardly
know what grief is.  The fresh wound may

be sore and deep, but if not mortal it heals. It's the wounds of the old that fester, and, wound following wound, that breaks the heart, and carries down the grey hairs with sorrow to the grave. My father! oh! my father! what has he not suffered? His son and heir, who might have been a protector to us in this troubled time, ill-fated in his bridal, distracted in after years, and flung to sudden death in some mental reverie of his own, or panic of his horse! And noo me, his daughter, whom he fondled, and for whom he yearns, filling up the cup of his misery, it may be, to overflowing. O! Margaret, the thought is more than my heart can bear."

"May God bless and strengthen your good father," said Margaret, the whole fervour of her religious principle aroused at the sight of this agony of spirit, "and may He cover you, too, Martha, in His pavilion! Dinna be too much cast down —dinna, dear Martha, I hae a forecast thae troubles will no last lang. I canna think that a haill country-side is to be turned upside doon, and the sacred feelings of a', high and low, young and auld, broken and champed in this gate by a pack o' scoonerils withoot either heart or conscience! 'The Lord reigneth on the earth.' See what assurance the Word gives us. As that sun issued out of darkness this morning, so the hand of the Almighty will issue from the dark cloud and bring deliverance to His suffering ones."

"I go away to-morrow," observed Martha, after some silence, " and I will go to the hills. It may be hoping against hope, but it is the only course open to me under Providence, and I cannot say I fear, whatever the consequences may be to myself. I fear more for what may happen

where I have been than where I am going
to.   But here is a token, Margaret," slip-
ping from her forefinger a gold ring in
which there was a setting of precious
stones.  " I value it much," added Martha,
" and have worn it since I was fifteen.   It
was given me by the good Christian woman
at Kirkinner, who said it had been a gift
to her when a maiden.   'There's no a
diamond in it, my lady,' she said to me—
' they're only natur gems;' and with a
smile, pointing to the various colours of
the stones, she added, ' There is the jasper,
there the amethyst, the emerald, the beryl,
the topaz—a' the stones ye read of in the
Revelations adorning the walls of the Holy
City to come.'   When I showed it to my
father he said that from so saintly a woman
it was as good as a sealing ordinance, and
told me to wear it as a memorial of Heaven.
Let me leave it with you, Margaret; and if

you should any time see Mrs. Lachlison or
Sir David they will know that you are dear
to me, and will receive you as they would
receive me."

Margaret took the ring, and said, with
some pleasantry, she hoped she would live
to restore it to Martha's finger above
another ring.

Next morning Martha joined the family at
breakfast like one prepared for a journey.
Margaret was also in attire of some readi-
ness for a convoy. The sky was grey and
cloudy, and as Margaret opened the casement and looked down the country as if
canvassing the prospects of the weather,
she heard a sound that startled her a little,
but she made no remark. When Glenvernoch came in, had sat down and said grace,
and the breakfast was proceeding, Martha
observed that she thought it was going to
be rain; but the farmer, with the weather-

wisdom of much observation and experience, said, " No ; the wun's high. It will blaw aff and be a fine day."

" The callan has been talking," he added after a while, " aboot an unco tooting and drumming at the Castle this morning; but there's nae sign o' ony mairch. A parcel o' idle loons—they'll nae doot be haddin some feast or rejoicing at expense o' the laird in honour o' the King, or Clavers, or some other sanct in their calendar."

On which remark Mrs. Wilson became a little nervous, and rose and looked out of the window. On the wind she thought she heard a strain of brazen music, and turning round to Margaret said, " Did ye hear onything ? "

" Yes, mother," said Margaret, rising ; " I heard it, and I think I ken what it is. Come, Martha. Ye're in gude time yet, but better to be aforehan'." And Martha

withdrew hurriedly with Margaret to her
room.

"Gudewife," said Glenvernoch, in some
consternation, "the sodgers canna be
coming here surely after lady Martha.
What should be done, think ye?"

But there had been little time for delibe-
ration when the young women reappeared,
mantled, and ready for the road—Martha
having under her mantle two velvet pouches
suspended from a morocco leather band
round her waist, and Margaret carrying a
well-strapped bag, containing the remainder
of Martha's wardrobe. The young lady
kissed Mrs. Wilson and Agnes, stroked with
her palm the cheek of Thomas, who had
stayed at home this morning, and then addressing the farmer, said, "Glenvernoch, I
could not desire a better protector than you,
or a happier home than yours, and if my
stay here should be a cause of trouble to

you or yours, forgive me, forgive me—will
ye forgive me?"

"Dinna speak aboot it, lady Martha,"
said Glenvernoch. "I'd rather stan' up
and fecht for ye at ance than pairt in this
hurry. It's a' nonsense."

"Come, Martha," said Margaret, who
had advanced to the front door; and the
farmer and Martha at once followed this
clear and decisive voice.

Glenvérnoch, on passing out through the
farm lane, expressed his doubts whether it
was prudent for Margaret to go with Martha.
If the soldiers should come, her absence
would only raise suspicions. Would it not
be better to send Sandy with lady Martha?
But this line of policy, though it had some
recommendations, was speedily overpowered
by the contrary reasoning of the young
women. "Dinna fear, faither, I'll be back
directly." "Besides," added Martha, " it

is better that Sandy, though a faithfu' man, should not know hoo I take my journey." And when Glenvernoch saw how nimbly they skipped over the stones in the stream he cried over to them, " Certes, ye're twa clever queens. Gude be wi' ye baith!" " But Maggie, wean," he added, as they smiled and waved their hands to him, " dinna be lang in coming hame."

The path of Martha and her companion on this occasion differed little from the course they had pursued two days before. When they had approached the Crag, Margaret said, " Whareaboots is the lad to be ?" " I think I will find it," replied Martha, " but we do not go down into the hollow. It is roon this way."

And Martha led round the other side of the ridge along rough and broken ground till they came to a straggling ascent between heavy boulders and projecting rock.

When the country north of the Crag came in view, Martha stopped, and said, "It is somewhere here," and, looking round, beckoned Margaret to follow, as she passed quickly down a little steep in the hill-side, where they presently found themselves shut out from the day-light and enclosed by rocks. Martha took a silver whistle from her bosom, and blew it, turning her ear eagerly to the darkness for a response, which immediately came in a whistle of the natural organ—one of those long-drawn whistles which almost speaks, and which every one hearing knows to be a signal. "That is it," said Martha, with much joy. "Willie never fails me ! Let us move back, dear, to the light."

They were followed in a few minutes to a level part of the ground by a young serving-man, driving a rough pony before him and leading a saddle horse. Martha

and Margaret had an affectionate farewell
in the somewhat uncertain hope of seeing
each other occasionally at the Sabbath services at the Caldons, Margaret observing, in
reply to the invitations of Martha, that it
was a commanded duty to assemble together
for Divine worship, and it was a duty the
peaceable observance of which she did not
own the right of any earthly power to for-
bid. "Though ye ken, mistress Martha,
I mauna press my faither's back ow'r hard
to the wa'."

# CHAPTER III.

'Ho! The king's redcoats are without,'
    The warder cried, in note full clear ;
'Well, let us stand to our redoubt,'
    The Chief replied, and shook his spear.
                    *Comic Almanac.*

MEANWHILE, as Margaret was returning to Glenvernoch, events of importance were occurring there. The farmer had been early informed by his picket that a small party of foot soldiers and a few horsemen were marching quietly up the country from Castle Stewart; and thus warned, he took his own procedure with customary energy and shrewdness.

" Sandy, gang ye and put the padlock and

crossbar on the yett. It will haud them awee till they gie us a challenge in proper military order. There's ower muckle water in the burn this morning for fitmen to think o' wading as lang as they hae a way dry-shod. As for you, Tammas," turning to his son, " ye'll better mak' yoursel' scarce, my man. Ye wad be shure to say something indiscreet, and maybe get into a fecht. Rin awa' ower the muir as fast as ye can to Kircailie, and tell them that the hairst wark is getting on sae weel that I think I'll be able to tak' delivery o' the lambs in a week or twa. Ye may rest there a day or sae, and see that the lambs are getting their meat. Noo, Bess (the kitchen-woman), and you, Dora (the byre-woman), ye'll hae to be strapping workers the day abune a' days. Dinna staun glowring at the sojers and their braws, and dinna answer ony questions. If ye get into question and

answer wi' them, they'll hae ye aff in chains
to Wigtown, and likely send ye as slaves to
the plantations. Tell them a', the captain
himsel', to staun oot o' your gate till
your wark's dune, and aye hae plenty o'
wark and mair o't in han'."

Thus, Glenvernoch, in the course of a
few minutes, had inspired his servants, male
and female, with a surprising sense of in-
dustry and conversational reserve. They
were for that day at least to be one of the
busiest communities ever seen on a farm,
and to carry the day gallantly by sheer dint
of the superiority of daily labour, and of
people attending to their own business, over
all military, official, or public interference.

In a closet interview with his wife the
farmer was no less decisive and deliberate.
" Sure to be much speering at us, gudewife,
about Martha Dunbar, whan we saw her
last, in what circumstances, whar she gaed

to, and sic inquisitions. We need tell nae
lees about seeing or enterteening lady Martha. The gentle lassie had the order of the
Government to leave Baldoon, and gang
onywhere else she liked, till within the last
twa or three days. I'll mak' a clean breest
to them o' a' this, tho' they may'na like it
vera weel. But noo, gudewife, say you
little or naething. Steer yoursel' aboot,
and get a gude denner ready—ane o' the
largest pats o' broth—I think it should be
the big washin' pot—with twa or three o'
your pickled quarters o' mutton, and look
oot some o' yer best yill. Thae fellows hae
been leeving at heck and manger in the Castle, and I'm much mista'en if they dinna
value gude eatin' and drinkin' mair than ony
other dooty they hae here."

On delivering this legal and culinary ex-
hortation to his wife, and seeing his instructions generally taking effect about the

steading, Glenvernoch cried to his man of all work, " Come awa wi' me, Sandy, and bring the key o' the padlock alang wi' ye" —not that Glenvernoch had anything for himself or Sandy at that particular juncture to do beyond moving to a certain post of observation, and being at some distance with the view of gaining time and thought.

" Hae ye seen onything forbye aboot the toon this morning, Sandy—ony comings or gangings oot o' ordinar worth mention ? " asked the farmer.

" Deil haet hae I seen, maister, that I wad crack ower my thoom at ony time," replied Sandy.

" That's weel, man, for whan meelitary come aboot the fairm toons they're unco keen for a' folk to see things whether they hae een or no. But, bliss me, Sandy, what's the callant jumping and waving sae daft-like on the bank for ? He'll be seen by the sojers, the stupid cratur, when he should be lying on his back, herding."

Sandy and his master scanned eagerly the track along the heugh, at some points of which travellers became visible.

" Ay, there they come noo," said Glenvernoch, " ane, twa, three—sax horse, and an officer, ane o' them, nae doot, a trumpeter. Brawly but soberly they ride, and in nae great hurry, covering the infantry. Dae ye see ony foot yet, Sandy ? "

" No a hoof or hide dae I see," said the farmer's man. " But aye, maister—aye ! I see the horses are breaking into a trot, or maybe a canter."

" It's that wullicat wi' his louping and signalling, when he should hae been as quate as pussy. But never heed, Sandy. The horses are no the kind to loup a dyke withoot a gallop stracht in the face o't, and that they canna afore oor yett. We'll wait the summons, and look awee for the infantry. I wad like weel to ken the strength o' the infantry."

Sandy counted a whole company, but finally reduced the number to ten, as far as he could distinguish.

" And a corporal," added Glenvernoch.

" An unco airmy to come on a bit fairm like this," added the farmer in a serious mood. " I wad rather hae twenty horse than ten infants, as they ca' them, at ony time. The horse are here the ae hour and awa' the next, but the infants settle doon like locusts on a place," the farmer was adding, when a trumpet sent its shrill blast through the air.

" That's the first toot, Sandy," said Glenvernoch, " but there maun be three toots, and ye'll hae time to gang doon and tak' oot the crossbar—leave wi' me the key o' the padlock, and mak' a' excuses, thrang

o' hairst time, needcessity o' keepin' wan-
neril beests oot o' the inclosure, likelihood
that the maister has the key o' the padlock in his pocket, gane ower the burn, but
nae doot has heard the summons like yersel',
and wal be there directly—in short, Sandy,
keep the haill army, horse an' foot, at the
yett till I gang doon."

When Glenvernoch arrived at the gate
of his inclosure, Sandy was in full palaver
with the officer of the party, the corporal's
guard of foot by this time being also on
the spot.

"I am Sergeant-Major M'Callum," said
the officer, with a document in his hand,
"on rather an unpleasant errand."

"Glad to see you, sergeant-major,
replied the farmer. "I hope there be
naething sae very unpleasant. But in ony
case," turning the key in the padlock, "it
would be very unceevil to keep ye a' stand-

ing there. Let me see your cartel,
sergeant-major."

"I will read it to you," said the officer,
proceeding to read his commission to
search the farmhouse of Glenvernoch and
its environs for Martha Dunbar of Baldoon, and to interrogate and examine the
farmer, Gilbert Wilson, and his wife, and
their daughter, named Margaret, and all
other competent witnesses on the said
farm, as to the whereabouts of the said
Martha, and her recent appearances there;
and if Martha Dunbar should be found, to
bring her forthwith to the Tolbooth of
Wigtown. Then followed a supplementary
instruction that as there was reason to
believe the notorious rebel and outlaw
William Hay, younger of Arioland, was
lurking within the bounds or on the
borders of the farm of Glenvernoch,
known to Martha Dunbar and Margaret

Wilson, all diligence was to be used in tracking his comings and goings with the folk of Glenvernoch, and that his capture or information tending to his capture, would be specially rewarded. " Signed Sheriff-Depute Graham in behoof and acting for John Graham of Claverhouse, Sheriff of Galloway in the King's name, Baron of Freuch, &c., &c." said the sergeant-major, holding out the document to Glenvernoch at the signature.

" I dinna doot ava sic a screed as that," said the farmer. " Hooever, as regards the main pursue, sergeant-major, ye're ower late o' coming, man. The bird's flown. But what's the use o' me havering here," flinging open the gate. " Sandy, lead up the sergeant-major's horse, whilom he and me talk on the business, and the party a' come up to the toon."

Sergeant-Major M'Callum, who himself

could not but think that this was the proper course of procedure, dismounted, gave his horse to Sandy, and ordering his men to follow up, walked with the farmer to the house.

When Glenvernoch led the officer into the parlour, he was saying rapidly, " Dinna speer or interrogat, or insist on answers to half a dizen questions at ance. This is my wife, sergeant-major M'Callum. Tak' a seat, sir; but, as I was saying, it doesna matter, noo at least, what day, or date, or 'oor a bird has flown. Your commission is to catch her. For my pairt I ken nae mair whaur she has flown than the man in the moon. Gif ye think ye can catch her, ye can flee aifter her, and I hae nae mair to say. But I'll no bide to be made a leear in my ain hoose, and I bin' you doon, as I said, to the first order in your cartel that you are to search thae premises for Martha Dunbar. When that point is cleared up, I'll answer your inter- rogats to the best o' my kenning. Noo, gudewife, show the sergeant-major and ony o' his men he likes every nook and corner o' the hoose. I maun gang oot and see after the horses. There's bare stabling for them a', but they maun a' hae water and corn, and the men some yill and bannocks nae doot. But gin the time, Mr. M'Callum, ye hae searched the hallan, I'll be ready to take ye through the oothooses."

The officer, after posting sentries, pro- ceeded to search the house, without any farther result than convincing him that the naïve confession of the farmer as to the bird being flown must be true. The anxiety of the wife to open every place of probable concealment disarmed all sus- picion; but to his repeated questions

when Martha Dunbar had been at Glenvernoch and when she had left, Mrs. Wilson
only replied that it had all occurred very
lately. "I maun follow the goodman,"
she said, "in the time to answer questions
mair preceesly."

It was with some impatience M'Callum
was urgently pressed by Glenvernoch to
search the outhouses, the barnyard, the
peat-stacks, and the hen-house. "I
believe what you said, Glenvernoch."
"Na, but dinna believe me," said the
farmer, "See with your ain een. Seeing's
the only believing noo-a-days, and I can
tell ye, sergeant-major, there are some
queer cosies aboot thae auld biggings, as
I'll show ye, whar a lady, or twa or three
o' them, micht be stowed in a pinch." So
the sergeant-major allowed himself to be
pulled through the premises, till, utterly
weary of a fruitless search, he said, "I

E 2

stand at your first word, Glenvernoch.
Mistress Dunbar is gone. That's clear
enough. But you must tell me at once
when she left, and where she has gone.
I cannot waste time on so simple a
matter."

"Weel, weel," replied Glenvernoch,
"sin' ye hae come that length, we'll gang
back into the parlour, and maybe ye'll
believe noo what I say. But ye hae half-
choked me already, sergeant-major, by
attempting to knock my honest word doon
my throat."

When the business was reopened in the
parlour, after some slight refreshment
ministered to the sergeant-major by Mrs.
Wilson, attended by her younger daughter
Agnes, Glenvernoch opened the diet in a
very conclusive spirit.

"Noo, Mr. M'Callum, as I understan',
ye wad ken whan lady Martha was here

and whan she gaed awa. I'll no tell ye
that to day or 'oor exactly, for a reason ye
are fit to judge. We had a veesit of your
superior, Captain Strachan, only twa or
three days syne, and he laid doon oor duty
in regard to lady Martha in expleecit
terms. I tauld her what the Captain had
said, that it was the will o' the authorities
that she return to Baldoon shure o' their
protection. And sae the young woman
left us, tacking her ain gate, because I'll
no be a public beagle, or a spy, or onything o' that sort, ye ken, sergeant-major
—that's no my business. I hae plenty o'
wark on my ain haudin', and neither laird
nor shirra maun think to make a naething
o' me. Bit a' this is neither here nor
there to your present commission, sergeant-major. What you wish to be at is
the precccse minnit lady Martha left Glenvernoch. That, to speak plainly, I'll no

tell ye, wi' a' respect, sergeant-major; for,
ye see, gin this should be a Shirra Coort or
Justiciar' affair the least wrang word o'
memory from you micht be as bad as
cutting my thrapple."

"Nonsense," said the sergeant-major,
laughing at a course of justice the possible
tragedy of which was a new idea to him,
having not before had a lecture of the same
kind, or much troubled himself about the
fate of those who fell under the law either
of his sword or his testimony.

"Naè sic nonsense," remarked the
farmer; "I hae heard o' as kittle things
turning on a bit question o' date afore noo.
But I tell you what, sergeant-major—I'se
no deny that had ye come yesterday
morning ye wad hae found lady Martha
here, and that's as near the wun' as I
can sail."

"Are you aware, Glenvernoch," said

M'Callum, " that William Hay was seen nae later than the day afore yesterday on your farm in company with Martha and your ain dochter?"

" I'm no sae shure o' that. At least, I neither ken nor hae heard ocht o' the kind. But I'll tak' my solemn aith," said Glen-vernoch, with decisive firmness, " that William Hay never crossed my doorstep in his life, nor has had communings far or near wi' ony o' my family, and I'll call on you, wife and dochter, and every ane aboot the place, to witness."

" There's a pass at the head o' the farm, on the Carrick side," said the soldier, as he rose, impatient for his saddle.

" Deed is there," said the farmer.

" I must ask you to show me the way to it."

" Shurely," said Glenvernoch, " but ye'll sit doon to your denner afore ye

mount. Gudewife, when will the denner
be ready for the strangers?"

But Sergeant-Major M'Callum declined
all delay, saying he would be back in
time, if not for dinner, for supper at least;
and after introducing Corporal Graw, of
the Foot, to Glenvernoch, as the officer in
charge during his absence, called his
horsemen and took the directions of the
farmer, who conducted the party down to
the gate, telling them to follow the tracks,
holding always to the left till the craggy
ridge came in view, "and when there,"
quoth the farmer, "ye can come back
doon on the ae side or the ither as ye may
choose."

"Sandy," said Glenvernoch to his man,
as they returned from the gate, "gang ye
ower the burn, and look for Maggie coming
hame, and warn her o' what has happened.
She's a prood, fearless thing, and would

come strapping in amang thae wild fallows
as if she were queen o' a' the land, maybe
·ask what they were doing here, and order
them awa. Bring her in quietly, Sandy.
Tell her I said it, and that she mauna
cross me."

The foot soldiers had stalked their arms
in front of the farm-house, and, in default
of other duty, were amusing themselves in
the street at pitch and toss, leap-frog,
and vain attempts to strike up an ac-
quaintanceship with the byre-woman and
other serving damsels. Bess of the kitchen,
as often as she had occasion to show herself, was a privileged person, the soldiers
to a man perceiving that she was engaged
in important duties. The ample dinner
reduced this military rabble to some degree
of order, Corporal Graw having the honour
of sitting with the farmer and his wife and
daughter at the upper end of the kitchen.

Dinner over, Glenvernoch, who had remarked to the Corporal at table that some
harmless amusement must be found for so
many idle men, rather astonished the officer,
while the latter was walking alongside
the arms, picking his teeth, when he came
out from the brew-house with a bundle of
fishing rods, lines, and hooks, saying,
" Here, lads, the burn's in richt fettle the
day for troot-catching. Fish doon the burn
awee, lads, till the sergeant-major comes
back aboot supper time. The farther ye
gang doon ye'll get the bigger troots. But
ye mauna gang far, as the Corporal will
tell ye. Hae, Corporal, divide the fishing
wands amang them, and let them play
themselves awee." The Corporal, after his
first surprise, could not but admit the pro-
priety of the arrangement, and most of his
guard were sent to fish down the stream.

Sergeant-major M'Callum, on returning

from his reconnaissance about sunset, sent forward a dragoon to order Glenvernoch and Corporal Graw to meet him at the gate.

"I must hurry on," he said to the farmer, "but Corporal Graw will wait with his men, and keep guard on the place till further orders."

The farmer, to whom this disposition was by no means welcome, replied, "If that's to be the gate, the men maun pit up in the shed for the nicht. Ten men are nae sma' lodging, sergeant-major, in a bit fairm-house without notice."

"There's nae ither way o't," said the dragoon officer. "Corporal Graw will keep his men in order;" and after a few private words to the Corporal, M'Callum and his horsemen rode off.

## CHAPTER IV.

Here comes Monsieur Le Beau; with his mouth
full of news.

*As You Like It.*

NEXT day Sheriff-depute Graham gathered
a little council of war round him.   There
were Major Winram, and Lagg who had
crossed a ford of the Cree, and ridden into
the county town during the morning from
Machermore Castle, turned of late into a
military head-quarter.   It was occupied by
the Earl of Home, commander of the Merse
Militia, on the arrival of his corps in the
district; and there Grierson of Lagg, on
returning from one of his inquisitorial raids

in the Stewartry, had an opportunity of meeting Claverhouse on his way to Newton and Kenmure Castle, when Allan Peerie and the reader last parted from the great man. The business of the council, to which Lagg had now been summoned by the Sheriff-depute, was to receive and consider the report of Sergeant-major M'Callum from the upper district of Penninghame.

The Sergeant-major described what had occurred at Glenvernoch, the search he had made of the premises, the admission of the farmer that Martha Dunbar had been in the house the previous day, but that he did not think it any part of his duty to detain her, and would give no information, or professed not to know, where she had gone. Otherwise the conduct of the farmer and his wife had been respectful and hospitable. The Sergeant-major did not conceal from the Council the strong and emphatic disavowal by Glenvernoch of any knowledge of Hay, and while thinking that the circumstances were in general suspicious, suggested that on this point the farmer might be sincere unless he were prepared to forswear himself. He then reported his ride through the upper part of the farm. He had seen or met with no one, though he discovered footmarks where the encounter between Hay and Picardy was said to have occurred. " On the grass near the head of the ravine," he said, " I found this," taking from his breast a small white cambric handkerchief, on a corner of which was sewn in blue thread the letters " M. W.," and added that near the same spot a bunch of newly-plucked heather-blossom was strewn on the ground. The Council would probably consider these traces as so far corroborative of Picardy's statement.

The Council approved of the discretion

of the Sergeant-major in leaving a guard
at Glenvernoch, and the members had
begun to give vent to their irritation at the
conduct of the farmer in allowing Martha
Dunbar to leave without giving notice at
least to the authorities, which could have
been done by a message of only a few miles
to Castle Stewart, when a dragoon rode up
to the door of the Sheriff's residence with
the following despatch from Claverhouse to
his brother, the Sheriff-depute :—

" Newton of Galloway.

"The rebel Hay made an attemp to
assassinat me last night, but compleatly
failed in his desine, tho' the roge made
good his escape in the darknes.   It will be
prudent not to appeir to be hard on the
old dame of Arioland, his mother, meantime.   Let her have better diet and beding
than other prisoners, and such privileges

as may be consistent with safe detention and strict watch and ward of her. By playing with the dam we may draw her cub into the toils.

(Signed)     " J. G."


This despatch fell like a bombshell on the council-table, echoed in fearful oaths and imprecations from the coarse lips of Lagg, and led to the immediate issue of a summons on Gilbert Wilson, farmer, to appear before the Sheriff-depute in the Court-house next day at noon, on pain of heavy fine for non-appearance. It also recalls our attention to the movements of Hay and Allan since we saw them withdrawing for consultation at midnight into the cave on the outskirts of Glenvernoch Farm.

## CHAPTER V.

And dar'st thou then
To beard the lion in his den,
  The Douglas in his hall ?

*Marmion.*

ALLAN returned before dawn to the shed at the farm-house, and threw himself down on the straw, more to stretch himself at full length than to sleep or repose. Hay, on the first streaks of daylight, led his horse out of the cavern, and rode rapidly off towards the hills. Their engagement was to meet the following day at the southern end of Loch Dee, or, if that rendezvous should fail, at the rowan-tree above Newton after dark.

Allan, in the early hours of the morning, entered the town of Monygove in his disguise as " Peerie." He was too conscious of the danger of frequent attendances on Claverhouse to have any desire to press himself on the attention of the captain of the host on this occasion. The feat required so much acting and self-command that he felt his life depended on an accident, and that he might be shot down at any moment if Clavers should be in one of his fiery tempers, or happen to be not too well pleased with the antics of his favourite fool. But at Machermore castle Claverhouse was a mile and a half from the town. It was unlikely he would make his appearance there before mid-day. As " Peerie," Allan would have the advantage of showing himself in the forenoon to the soldiers and some of the officers, who, if Clavers, after the entertainment he had

had the previous day, should inquire after
him, would be able to inform their chief
that the fool had been wandering about the
streets an hour or two ago. Barnkirk, for
which Allan had taken an unceremonious
departure from Claverhouse the previous
day in search of broth, was close to Monygove, on the other bank of the Cree. The
journey from Monygove to Newton was
twenty miles, through a wildly pastoral
and mountainous district, not particularly
attractive to a fool who had to keep pace
on foot with the dragoons, with no inns
and few farm-houses on the way. If all
this should fall into the mind of Clavers
he would laugh, and see in it only another
proof of the natural food-instinct and
mother-wit of Allan Peerie. Suspicion
would so far be again disarmed. Another
advantage Allan promised himself was that
in Monygove he would pick up news, hear

or overhear much of the talk of Clavers'
followers, and particularly whether the
order of march would proceed as it had
been fixed the previous day.

These purposes having been accomplished
to Allan's satisfaction, he suddenly disappeared from the old market-place, swarming
at this period much beyond its powers of
reception with soldiers, horse and foot, its
central square covered with rude tents and
booths, and its few taverns ringing from
early morning to late at night. By what
road Allan disappeared no one knew. But
avoiding the more common track, and taking
bypaths abridging the whole distance, his
road was straight to Newton of Galloway,
in advance of Clavers twenty-four hours.
Nor had he advanced far, not more than
two or three miles, when entering a cot-
house as "Peerie" he came out from it
shortly in a different garb, and strode

forward.  He was here in a country where every farmer, every cottar and shepherd, was sullenly, if not actively, opposed to the state of affairs—many even chafing with rage, yet benumbed by the sense of helpless inaction which falls over people in solitary places—and, as he passed on through the defiles of Kitterick and Cragdhu, a country where many exiles and proscribed wanderers from other parishes were harboured, and deemed themselves, though without arms or organization, in a strong place.  To these Allan was a messenger of mercy.  He told them what was coming immediately behind him, and warned them to fall back from the dragoon tracks, to hide themselves, and let the vain and glittering hailstorm pass by.

This was the difficulty of Clavers in Galloway—the phantom enemy that seemed to disappear before him, yet was always at his side, and rose in his rear erect. "I can find few or no enemies here," he wrote in substance more than once to the Privy Council; "they are all so struck with terror." And yet the while he was biting his nails and gnawing his vitals in imbecile rage and conscious vexation that he had scarce a friend in the whole province.

Allan kept his rendezvous with Hay at Loch Dee, the attainment of which by the latter, indeed, across flat heaths and barren hills, along the edge of several wild tarns and over various streams, had been a work, though on horseback, of greater difficulty, accomplished as it had been for the most part over night, than had fallen to Allan on foot. Yet not far from where the Dee issues in no great volume from the loch of the same name they had a place of shelter and hospitality, and it was with renewed strength, and no little curiosity of spirit,

they sauntered out about mid-day to put
themselves behind some rocks overlooking
a point of the river where it widened
among black boulders and over a pebbly
bed into a mere strand, only to gather itself
together again a few paces farther down
into a deep, narrow pool between steep
ledges of rock. This ford Clavers' party
had to pass. And there, little behind the
time Allan had conjectured, came the
cavalcade, fifty horsemen, two abreast,
under a gloomy but retentive sky, only a
few heavy drops of rain falling amid fitful
gleams of sunshine, the wind tossing and
sweeping onward the black clouds, as if
playing with them in a sort of feline
mastery.

Hay looked eagerly from his point of
vision at the troop as they straggled down
in double file to the ford. "What an opportunity is here lost, Allan," he at length

said. "Why, twenty men could annihilate
the whole force, leaving Claverhouse to me.
What a fool Kenmure is to twiddle, equivocate, and connive in his strong castle to
his own ruin, when by holding up his finger
he could cut the throat of all this tyranny!"

"Ay," remarked Allan, "it would be
much easier wark here than at Bothwell.
But see Clavers! See how securely he
rides behind his horsemen, with twa or
three on each side o' him. See hoo he is
spurring forward! Faith, he's no to be
hindmost in crossing. He'll no bide this
side the water when his horse are on the
ither. See hoo keenly he looks afore and
ahint him, an' roon the corners o' every
big stane—hoo nervous!"

"The conscience-stricken coward," said
Hay. "He knows every blade o' grass in
Galloway is opposed to him."

"See, there he clatters through the stran'

amid a score o' them," continued Allan,—
" and noo through the shaws," referring to
thinly-scattered tufts of bushes which grew
along the other bank of the stream.

As the troop emerged from the thicket
and fell into order along the bare slope, a
broad flash of lightning clove the sky between them and the two secret onlookers,
brightening for an instant the helmets and
accoutrements of the dragoons, and followed
by a belching roar of thunder peculiar to
such mountainous districts.

" Heaven rebukes the scoundrels if men
will not," said Hay, as he sprang to his
feet, and threw a cloak round his shoulders,
under the rain now falling from the black
cloud over the ford. " What an opportunity
has been lost ! Oh ! Kenmure, Kenmure,
what you have to answer for to your country
and to your own house ! "

"Deed, Clavers' hash cood hae been nicely

settled here," quoth Allan ; " but from what
ye hae seen, Hay, he's no to be attacked
single-handed when on the march.    He is
ıane o' your knicht-errant gentry to accept
a fair fecht in the face o' his sojers, or ever
so mony fine ladies.    He seldom  draws his
sword or his pistol save to strike doon some
puir airmless Covenanter."

"What I have seen," said Hay firmly,
" has only strengthened my purpose, Allan.
I will brave that imp of darkness to his
beard, come what may."

After dark two men on horseback drew
up under an old rowan-tree on one of the
various tracks overlooking the hollow, in
which the bounds of the burgh of Newton
had been fixed by Royal Charter.    On the
" curple " behind one of the riders sat a
country lad in his teens.    Of the burgh
itself no sign was visible save a few vapoury
stalks of milky whiteness shot up into the

lark air from the lights of the hostelry and
the few houses around it. But between
the burgh and Kenmure Castle bright lights
shone through the trees, now parting rapidly
with their foliage, some lights steady, and
others flickering from one point to another.
The old baronial stronghold, on its green
mound, was more illuminated than usual;
and farther in the distance, under a clearer
part of the sky, points of starlight fell on
the waters of Loch Ken.

The riders were soon joined by a scout
from the burgh, who informed them that
Clavers had made the inn his headquarters,
was to sleep there, and after billeting the
troop had rode out in the gloaming to the
Castle, attended by two dragoons.

This agreed so well with the prognos-
tications of Allan that he said to the
lad behind his saddle, " Jump doon,
boy."

"Stay," said Hay, "let us know more. How have the troop been lodged?"

"There are sax in the inn stables, and as the folk in the toon hae had to pit oot their coos, there may be nearly sax mair scattered aboot. The men are to sleep in their claes at the toon-hoose. Some hae been sent to the manse, but the maist feck are in the Castle stables."

"What guards are posted?" inquired Hay.

"Nae guards at a'," replied the scout; "only twa troopers riding sentry at the tap o' the brae on the Dalry road. They're to be relieved in the nicht time by some o' the fallows frae the manse."

The lad now slid from the saddle, and, after receiving instructions from Allan, accompanied the scout down a by-way into the burgh.

Hay and Allan waited at the rowan-tree

till they had heard the tattoo beating the soldiers to night-quarters, and then rode boldly forward, avoiding the sentries, to the front door of the inn, where, on dismounting, their horses were taken by a prompt hostler, to whom Hay said, " Thankee, lad. They're no for the stable, ye ken; walk them up and doon a wee; we'll be oot directly"— in the tone of a countryman passing on to his farmhouse. "Come awa in, Jock, and hae some refreshment."

Master and man passsed into a little par- lour behind the staircase, allotted to way- farers. It might have had company, but on this evening it had none—the presence of Clavers rather forbidding the usual cus- tom of " the country parlour," as it was called. They were waited on, after some delay, by a wench who casually looked in, and seeing two men where she thought there had been none, recognized one of the two, for she said in a momentary surprise, " You, Mr. Hay, here the nicht ! "

" Quiet ! " said Hay, putting his finger on his lips, and advancing to the maid, added, " Nae idle talk, Nancy. Bring us a pint o' the best, and say naething to the maister or mistress about Hay or onybody else. We're twa country chiels wi' information to Clavers. Do ye understan' ? "

"I think I understan', Mr. Hay, tho' it mayna be very easy," replied Nancy, who, on returning with the pint, said, " The maister's oot aboot the stables, but I tauld the mistress, and there's the pint," as she held out her hand for the money.

There was a distinguished arrival soon after, which drew all to the front door. It was Clavers, attended not by the two dragoons only, but a considerable escort besides from the Castle. These, however, on Clavers alighting and entering his head-quarters, wheeled about and returned to the Kenmure stables. The landlord had conducted his guest up the staircase with every mark of distinction, and taken his orders for the night, when, on coming down, the hostess said, " Dear me, John, I had amaist forgot. The lassie said in the fore-nicht there were twa chiels in the parlour wi' despatches to the Captain."

" Captain! ye silly wife, he's a lord. He's Baron and Sherra-principal here, and mickle mair at Edinbro'. We maun see aboot that."

But on the two looking into the parlour there was nobody there—nothing but the stoup and glasses. " Havers!" was the ejaculation of the landlord, as he turned to other duties. " Sic a nicht as we'll hae, wife. Twa o' the force are to keep guard in the under-storey till daybreak, and a shakedoon is to be laid for the body servant

at the head o' the stair, forby a' the doors
and windows to be weel fastened. I see
I'll hae tae sit up a' nicht mysel'."

Hay and Allan had, in fact, disappeared
from the parlour sometime before the arrival
of Claverhouse.

Hay passed up the stair, and along a
lighted gallery, on one side of which
were the two principal apartments of the
inn, and at the other end a stair leading
down to a passage into the kitchen on one
hand and out into a vegetable garden on
the other. This back stair was unlighted.
The door of the first apartment was wide
open, a blazing fire in the hearth, and long
candles burning on the mantelpiece. The
door of the second apartment was more
than two-thirds closed, and the interior
lighted only by a taper in front of a small
mirror on the toilet table. Hay passed
into this second room. His eye caught two

small silver-mounted pistols on either side of the mirror. Both were loaded. He pushed one of the pistols between the breast buttons of his doublet, and forthwith shrouded himself in the ample curtain at the head of the bed within a yard of the door.

Claverhouse, on dismissing the landlord, and sending his servant to repeat to the serjeant-major the orders he had already given as to a guard in the hostelry, appeared to have little more to do that evening. He withdrew almost immediately to the bed-room, where his first act was to light the candles on the toilet table from the taper, and look into the glass. "Poor Kenmure," he said, twisting his moustache, "I have him round my finger," and admiring the proud curl of his lip, gave a little laugh, as if it could not possibly have been otherwise in presence of such a physiognomy. He then proceeded to undress, and had his crimson surtout half over his shoulders when he looked into the glass again, meditatively, and another thought came. "Kenmure did speak rather sharply on the subject of his old kinswoman of Arioland. What could he mean? Pshaw? salving his conscience, no doubt," and off went the laced coat. "But not a word did my lord say," continued Clavers, as he was easing his shirt of mail,—"not a word, my lord Ken, about her rebel son. That poor whelp is accursed of friend and foe." And the shirt of mail in a moment or two would have been hanging loosely over his silk jacket but for a sudden footfall in the apartment.

Clavers wore his sword, and on looking round there stood before him a tall, manly figure, also wearing a sword, its arms folded, and its eyes fixed upon

him, not without a glare of deadly fierce-
ness.

Clavers' first impulse was to rush to the
door, but Hay, flinging him back, said,
" Sir, do not be more alarmed than becomes
a man of honour."

Clavers clutched backward on the table
for his pistol, but as soon as he turned to
fire, Hay, having pulled the other pistol
from his breast, had the muzzle almost in
the mouth of his enemy, whose weapon
dropped out of his hand.

Hay, on the same instant, threw his pistol
on the floor.

" Man or devil; who art thou ? " gasped
Claverhouse, with as much whispering
breath as he could muster in his terror,
leaning with one hand on the table.

" John Graham," said the other de-
liberately, " I am William Hay, whom thou
pretendest to despise, for whose blood thou

hast been long thirsting like a stealthy tiger, and whose mother, thou pitiless beast, thou hast condemned as a slave to the plantations. No more words. Draw and defend thy life, villain!" cried Hay, his sword flashing from its scabbard.

Claverhouse was motionless. He stood a moment at bay, and then stared wildly round him.

"Draw and fight, or by the heavens above us I shall cut the head off your body where you stand," exclaimed Hay, the deed hanging on his words, when cries of "Murder! Assassins!" escaped from Claverhouse, as he pressed behind the table to open the window and sound his clamour to the night air, Hay advancing on him with the point of his blade.

In another moment Clavers might have been a dead man, but the words of Margaret of Glenvernoch, "Dinna lift the bluidy hand," came back on Hay's ears with all the piercing fervour on which he had first heard them, and were enforced by his own soldierly sense of honour. Three loud raps at the door also admonished him that his time was up. "Coward!" he said, striking his enemy in the face with the back of his hand, and withdrew from the room, the door of which opened before him under the fingers of Allan. The two escaped by the back stair, while the landlord was crying "Help! help!" at the front door, and the tramp of feet began to be heard mounting the front staircase. To rush through the garden, leap the hedge, find their horses, mount, and ride away over rough but silent ground was but the work of a few minutes; and Hay and his faithful henchman had gained the road towards Loch Dee before pursuit of any kind was possible.

## CHAPTER VI.

I will make a Star-Chamber matter of it.
*Justice Shallow.*

CLAVERHOUSE, as soon as freed from personal danger, recovered his customary
agility of command, to which the fierce
and active passion with which he was now
agitated lent additional impetus. He
roused every trooper in the burg, and while
sending off a party on horseback to search
the roads up Glenken, he ordered another
party on foot to ransack the houses and
their environs. Hay, if found, or any one
aiding him, he ordered to be shot down on
the spot, and brought to him dead or alive.

Meanwhile he interrogated keenly the inmates of the house. On the landlord he was particularly severe.

" Ho! mine host, is this the way you protect your guests, when not only the white wand, but the royal sceptre itself may be said to be over your door ? " To which question mine host could only reply with a shudder.

" You have no answer, Gordon, but tell me this. Would you know Hay if you saw him ? "

" Perfectly, your lordship," said the trembling innkeeper, "if I saw him. But I haena seen him, may it please your highness, as shure as I staun afore ye, and as I hae to answer for at the great day o' judgment."

" Cant! " exclaimed Clavers with fury. " Away with your snivelling appeals to the day of judgment! Are you sure of the truth of what you say before one who will judge you this moment?"

"Weel, I declare," said the landlord, "this is unco unceevil, my Lord Claver-hoose. Gude guide us, to think I should be act and pairt in a 'sassination in my ain hoose!"

"How did Hay come into the house without your knowing?"

"Wi' my kenning," replied the inn-keeper, "that hae sae mickle business ootby, providing corn and hay for the horses and up-pitting for the men. Besides, wha in their mortal senses wad hae jaloosed that sic an ootlaw and ne'er-do-weel could hae come boldly in to your verra head-quarters on sic a deadly errand? A' my kenning aboot the matter is what the lassie said, no to me indeed, but to her mistress in my absence, and that was, that a farmer or drover and his man cam in, and had a refreshment, for which they paid doon the siller, and were aff again in a jiffy, naebody caring or looking mair after them."

"Bring the lass here," said Clavers, determined to confront the witnesses.

When Nancy appeared, though in some disarray, having at the close of the turmoil thrown herself down on her bed-cover, and almost fallen asleep, Clavers, eying her closely, appeared to see some comeliness in the country girl.

"Certes, Nancy, ye're a good-looking queen, say who will to the contrary. I should not be surprised if you were in love with Master Hay, or Master Hay with you, in which case it will be as difficult to get the word of truth out of your mouth as to draw blood from a millstone."

The girl, blushing at this crafty but not unpleasing suggestion, held down her head, with one of her fingers between her lips.

" But now, Nancy," continued Clavers, " say truly like an honest lass, was Hay one of the two men whom ye served with liquor, as your master says ? "

" He micht be," said the waiting-maid of the Newton Inn on this eventful occasion, " or he micht be no, sir. If it wasna him, it must hae been Tam Picardy, the Wigtown cattle-dealer. There were twa o' them, sir. I didna look at them baith mair than half a minute, and ane's een couldna be very stracht atween the twa in sic a short blink."

" Come now, Nancy, the blink was not quite so short as ye pretend. It is not so pretty country wenches like you deal with gallant visitors on an evening."

" We were a' ow'r thrang in the house, sir, for ony jinking. It's the truth I'm telling you, I didna see them mair than half a minute ony time, and in twa or three minutes mair they were gane, and their horses frae the door. For I looked oot and saw they were na there, and my mistress kens the truth of what I'm saying."

"Your wife, Gordon?" said Clavers interrogatively, as if the landlady must now appear also as a witness.

"My wife, my gudewife," said the innkeeper, "bless me, I haena been thinking o' her in a' this worry as I should hae been. She fainted clean awa', your lordship, on the first hullabaloo; never recovered indeed; and as she's in a delicate condition ony gate it may gang, she'll likely come waur oot o' this dreedfu' affair than onybody else."

As orderly after orderly now began to enter the' state-room with reports of the failure of the search, Claverhouse suddenly prorogued this diet of examination; and assured at length of the escape of Hay, he sat down and wrote the highly-coloured report of attempted assassination to the Sheriff-depute, of which the reader has been already apprised, and in which there was so strange a mixture of policy and passion. The despatch sent off, he gave the necessary orders for a raid in force through Glenken as soon as the sun should give light to see such fugitives as might be beaten up, and to track them to their hiding-places. A fresh party of dragoons were ordered up from Kenmure stables, while those who had been fagged by night duty were left in guard at the inn; and soon after dawn, men and horse refreshed, their leader chafing between mortified pride and eager thirst of vengeance, the troop sallied out from the little town in gallant order.

Rapid as Clavers' movements had been,

tidings of what had transpired over night had passed along the glen before him. The solitary strath, as he advanced, was more quiet even than usual. The roads were totally deserted; the farm-houses seemed reposing in Sabbatic cessation from labour; there were no reapers in the late cornfields, no hay-makers gathering up the remains of winter fodder. Only a wide valley with broken slopes of pleasant pasture on either side, where some sheep and cattle might be seen, but no human being. Only on distant uplands some sign of labour might be caught, but these had to be approached with caution. The plan adopted by Claver-house on such occasions was to send detachments from the main party to as many of the farm-houses as could be reached without departing from the general operation, to interrogate, search, and frighten the inmates; the chances would then be that any fugitives or outlaws hanging loosely about the various steadings would be shaken off on the first approach of the dragoons, and, thus driven into the open within a circle of pursuing troops, be finally earthed in some morass.

Claverhouse crossed the Ken with the main part of his force, and ordered the other to advance along the right bank to the ford, some few miles up the river, the whole troop to draw together at the village of Dalry—the scene in past years of a successful feud of the people against a small party of soldiers, which had been the signal of the Pentland rising, and a place of ill repute to Clavers and all his faction ever since.

Dalry was silent as the grave when Clavers and his dragoons entered. Every door of the straggling hamlet was closed. The curiosity even of the women and children seemed to be wholly quenched. No one was seen looking out of the windows. Near the top of the broad street, by which Dalry was building itself in some order over the hill-face on which it was scattered, a tall, large-headed man, with marks of intemperance quivering along the nerves of a red and blown face, but, on the whole, of a grave and thoughtful aspect, was seen looking over his half-door. Here the troop halted, and Clavers, riding up to the door, accosted the shop-keeper.

" Ye're very quiet here to-day, Rorison," he remarked.

" Very quiet, your honour," replied the shopkeeper ; " it's the Fast-day."

" What mean ye by the Fast-day ? No preachings or conventicles, I hope."

" Oh! no, naething o' that kind here for mony a lang day. It's a mere fashion the bodies hae, aye when the

memory o' Rullion Green or the expulsion
o' the auld minister comes roon. They
think they're no richt unless they show
some respect to what was ance a great
doonfa' to them, and this is the wye they
respect the day, your honour—close their
doors and a' sit doon on their hunkers,
stoopid craturs!"

Claverhouse, pressing his lips, suddenly
turned the conversation. "Have you seen
two men passing through within the last
half-hour, Rorison?"

"No, I'm sure no. If they are fugy
they wad hardly come this gate wi' dragoons
at their heels. Mair like they wad haud
roon the Moniaive direction. But while
the horses are resting, gif your honour
shood step in—ye see I hae my shutter up
like the lave o' them—there's really naething to be dune in the clachan on a Fast-day
but to refresh—and I'll be glad to gie ye

ony information, as weel as a drap o' the best in my bottle."

Claverhouse, not expecting further information from this source, declined the hospitable invitation of the shopkeeper, and after detailing searching parties to go round the houses, rode down himself towards the ford, and from a bluff at the lower end of the village, looking over a stretch of corn and meadow ground, saw his troopers crossing the shallows of the Ken.

The officer in command of this detachment reported that they had started three fellows, who appeared extremely anxious to keep at a distance. One of them had doubled on his pursuers by clambering behind a rocky precipice, where neither horse nor foot could follow him; and while pressing after the others they had lost sight or trace of them while beating the woods

within a short distance of the ford. The
fugitives must either have crossed the river
or be pressing their way under cover to
Carsphairn.

"S'death on you," said Claverhouse;
"why not track them, and make sure of
one event or the other?"

"Pardon me, General," answered the
subaltern, giving an expression to the
military title of his leader common among
his troopers—"I have left a guard on the
other side with that intention, and to receive further orders at the ford."

This arrangement seemed to appease
the tactical cravings of Clavers, and in a
short while the troop were again on the
circuit—the party which had crossed the
ford advancing along the course of the
river, with orders to trend their line of
march towards the moorland between
Glenken and Moniaive, while their chief

and the rest of the force made a wider sweep round Dalry towards the same rendezvous.

It was mid-day when the two parties came in view of each other on one of those upland heaths which, though of broken and unequal surface, are like level plains uplifted between the hills. Both were conscious of having prey before them, and had followed the fugitives as they sped across the morass till the movement of the latter was scarce distinguishable from the wings of the plovers which rose from the heather, and screamed in circling flights as these unaccustomed figures strode through the covers. The notion that Hay might be among the number fired the blood of Clavers. But they were beyond the approach of cavalry. Yet they were equally beyond any place of absolute refuge or secure retreat. A number of the troopers were dismounted and sent forward into the depths of the morass, while the horsemen were spread out in wings round the advancing footmen.

At length five crouchers were dragged from a peat hag fossed by pools of water as prisoners of war to Clavers. They were all of the peasant or small farmer class, and unarmed. But they were men of such stern conviction and hardened passion that, when questioned, no arms in the world could extract from them a complying answer. Had they taken the Test? No. Would they take the Test now? Never! Clavers, departing from this well-worn formula, impatiently demanded whether they knew William Hay? Would they swear they had never seen or heard of him? When had they seen or heard of him last? To all which interrogatories the prisoners simply shook their heads, some with a smile,

others with a visible expression of con-
tempt towards the querist.

" Curse the rascals ! " cried Claverhouse.
" They are all of the same pack; shoot
them down ? "

And the contents of a dozen carbines
immediately passed through the bodies of
these recalcitrants.

" Shall we bury them ? " asked the
lieutenant, on returning from the bodies
quivering in their last agonies.

" Bury them ! " replied Clavers. " Why
waste time in burying such carrion ? The
corbies and the eagles "—pointing to birds
of prey already hovering over the ghastly
scene—" are our sextons. To horse ! all
to horse ! "

The troop returned in a brisk march
towards the Ken, crossed the ford, picked
up the guard, and entered the burgh of
Newton before dark with an air of fatigue.

But Claverhouse did not retire to much-needed rest that evening without paying a visit to Lord and Lady Kenmure at the Castle.

## CHAPTER VII.

Friendly free discussion calling forth
From the fair jewel Truth its latent ray.
*Thomson.*

THE visit of Claverhouse, though expected by Kenmure, occurred under different circumstances from what had been
contemplated.   There had been some fore-
shadow in the conversation of the previous
evening of an arrangement by which the
Viscount hoped to protect his friends and
relatives under doom of law, as well as to
secure his estates from military invasion
on his becoming responsible for the good
behaviour of his tenantry and dependents,

engaging that they should not take arms,
speak evil of the curates, or obstruct the
established authority.    Claverhouse had
humoured this design, without admitting
its consistency with the policy either of
himself or his superiors, and insisted as a
condition that Kenmure, if his example
were to have due weight in the country,
should give a full adhesion to the measures
of the Government—an adhesion implying
not a mere passive submission to the Test
Act, but an active co-operation in its
enforcement, to which the Viscount could
not assent.    Yet a temporary accommodation seemed not impossible.    It was Kenmure's belief that as soon as the eyes
of the King were opened to the cruelties
and miseries inflicted by his agents in
Scotland, and saw how completely they
were tearing up the roots of the Royal
authority in his ancient kingdom, a great

change would take place in the administration of affairs ; and any temporary accommodation, for which he was willing to
make some sacrifices, that should tide over
the brief interval, consequently appeared
to him adequate to the occasion. But the
affray in the inn on the previous night
was felt on both sides to have transported
this delicate negotiation into a new atmo-
sphere. The tidings had been early carried
to the Castle, blazoned in all the scarlet
colours of attempted assassination in which
Clavers had traced them, and assuming
every hour a darker hue in the gossip of
the populace and the stables. What the
events of the day had been were yet un-
known in the Castle. But Clavers' raid in
force could have borne no good fruits, and
was in the last degree unwelcome to Kenmure. For whatever alarm, injury, or
bloodshed it had caused he would be

blamed by his retainers, and would fall
still lower in their esteem than he had yet
fallen.

Lady Kenmure received her guest with
a visible agitation, which, if it comported
sympathy for the danger to which his life
had been exposed, was not the less free of
fear for the violent and revengeful spirit by
which he was well known to be actuated.
Kenmure greeted Claverhouse with formal
politeness, but was demure, and almost
silent.

At table, in presence of the domestics,
the conversation was of the most general
and reserved character. Claverhouse, in a
congratulatory tone, remarked on the quiet-
ness of the district. It was difficult to
believe, he said, that the assassin Hay was
not under hiding in the neighbourhood,
but he vowed to Kenmure, with apparent
satisfaction, that beyond that vile des-

perado himself there were not now in
Glenken half-a-dozen enemies of the public
peace. Lady Kenmure rose early, and in
conducting her from the table Claverhouse
said that in the business with my lord
he would like her ladyship to be present.
She would receive them together at their
pleasure in her withdrawing-room was the
lady's reply.

" What is the exact relation, Captain
Graham, of this audacious attack of Hay?
What was his object? How did he
escape? The reports are so unintelli-
gible."

" His object, my dear Lord Kenmure,
was to slay your humble servant," said
Claverhouse, " and he fled, because while
thirsting for my life he was unwilling to
endanger his own."

" How was he armed and attended ? "

" He was armed with sword and pistols,

and had stealthily bestowed himself alone
in the curtains of my bed.   It is a miracle
I escaped."

"Did he fire?"

"No."

"Did he strike?"

"No."

"Did he make himself known to you?"

"He did."

"Why did you not fall upon him?
You had your arms, your people at hand—
the whole house in which to contain him?
You have lost a rare opportunity of securing
an outlaw whose recusancy is made the
pretext of pursuing to the last extremities
his whole kith and kin.   As for the young
man, knowing nothing of arms but what he
has picked up in the sports of the country,
I believe he must be mad to encounter in
this wild fashion such a master of fence
as Captain Graham.   If he did not lay

hands on you, why did you not seize him?"

Claverhouse, wincing, and feeling keenly the sting of these remarks of Kenmure, would have liked to break loose in some violent tirade; but restraining his passion, while drinking a cup of wine, he looked across the table, with an arch but haughty smile, as he said—" Poor Captain Graham, my good lord, has more to think of in this world than a master of fence. Were he to rush into single combat with every madman that crosses his path, his course would, no doubt, be as short as his worst enemies could desire. When he dies under arms I hope it shall be on the battle-field, whether amid the shouts of victory or the wail of defeat."

" There, on the other hand, you are too warlike," said Kenmure, lifting the wine to his lips in politeness to his guest.

"You are looking to civil war, when the great object is to avert it."

"Here, my lord, we approach the asses' bridge on which we have so often landed," replied Clavers good-humouredly, as he rose from the table. "How to avert civil war? Let us go to Lady Kenmure. She is the most amiable and the most reasonable lady I have found in Galloway—a noble contrast to the old shrew of Stair, Heaven bless her memory, for I hope she will now plague us no more."

"I was saying to my lord," said Clavers, after the first civilities, on taking a seat between the husband and the wife on the hearth of the drawing-room, "that the only way to avert civil war and bring peace to the country is a unanimous and decided stand of the chief men in favour of royalty and the established order of affairs.

The base commonalty, my lady, trade on the great houses. Every turn of the vane over the walls of the castles is watched, and the people disport themselves as they see how the wind blows one way or another. So the disorder is prolonged—never has an end. My lord's influence, so far as he has gone, must have been valuable. I have seldom seen a quieter district than Glenken. Yet would you believe, my lady, that we have to-day tracked and apprehended no fewer than five rebels and disturbers of the peace—rogues and vagabonds who would keep a country-side in uproar. A steady frown of my lord would frighten all these foul birds off the ground. I verily believe that even Hay, wild as he is, would not have dared to make his wicked attempt unless he had thought that the neighbourhood of Kenmure Castle was neutral ground. Deci-

sion of purpose is thus essential to bring
the troubles to an end, and I shall hope for
your kind graces, my lady, in pleading for
me with my lord to take a part worthy of
the chivalrous loyalty of his ancient race."

" You must bear in mind, Grizzel," said
Kenmure, " that our friend Claverhouse, in
this ardent speech, is discharging with
much ability the function of devil's advo-
cate. I believe he honestly does not see, or,
if seeing, does not wish to be seen, any side
of the question but his own. All from my
point of view is excluded from his argu-
ment. The country, this part of it at
least, can only be pacified by growing confidence that there shall be temperate coun-
sels and proceedings. On that condition
I could answer for the peace of the greater
part of the Stewartry, with such compli-
ance as the Government could reason-
ably look for in the present religious

differences. But were Kenmure to declare himself a headlong partisan of the Privy Council he would from that hour have no more moral influence than a parish beadle. Could he, even if he would, take horse and play the part of your kinsman Lagg, dame, you know as well as I do that so far from strengthening the hands of our gallant friend here he would only bring into the King's house seven devils worse than the first."

"And you also know, my lady," promptly rejoined Claverhouse, " how tender the Government has been through all this controversy, in which I am sorry my lord is so difficult to be moved; how they would have placed an ample garrison in the castle to support my lord's authority; and how they have refrained year after year to take forcible possession of a post so necessary to support the Royal dignity.

Queensberry in his letters insists on maintaining the local influence of the principal Barons, and never fails to mention Kenmure."

" Queensberry should remember the motto of his own house," said the Viscount dryly. " ' Better to hear the lark sing than the mouse cheep.' The mistake is in thinking that the Whigs, if put utterly to the wall, will not do as yourselves would do in like circumstances. They will leave you the castles, and all the mice and cats in the castles, and betake themselves to the hills and the woods like their ancestors, till they succeed or the common country be ruined. The bear may be killed, indeed, but there will be nothing left but the skin to quarrel over."

A contemptuous frown passed over the face of Claverhouse at these remarks of Kenmure.

"I am sure," said the lady, "we are much indebted to the Government for the respect to our estate, and if there is anything more we can do we should think of it favourably."

"Good, my lady," said Clavers, "why should not my lord do as your brother Galloway, and Castle Stewart, and Ravenstone, and Agnew, Garthland, Baldoon, and nearly all the barons in Galloway have done?"

"Why not, Kenmure?" asked the lady, with an eager and querulous light in her eyes as she fixed them on her husband.

"What have they done, Grizzel, which we have not done? We hold no conventicles, we encourage none, we advise and use what influence we have over the people to abstain from any overt violation of the decrees of the Privy Council. What more can any house in Galloway boast of?

I call the Sheriff himself to witness. You
have many testers, Graham, who have
swallowed the words out of your mouth as
they were given. But what have they
done for you? They have yielded you
their castles, or you have taken them.
But the men, the living epistles, remain
the same as they were before. Sir Andrew
has retired to his property in Ireland.
But he does not help you in your under-
taking a whit more from having taken
your Test. There shall be no hypocrisy
in my dealings with the Government. I
have no Ireland or any other refuge to run
to, and I do not mean to fly anywhere
from the place where I am. This castle
and these lands have come to me from my
ancestors, and I shall hold them in my
right, with an honest bearing, till I am
forcibly dispossessed of them."

"My lord," said Clavers, in a firm but

as frank and friendly a tone as he could assume, "it has been my unpleasant duty to explain to you so often what we would wish you to do that I must now ask, in the name of heaven, what you would have us to do?"

Kenmure rose, and rested his elbow on the mantelpiece. Clavers also rose, and Lady Kenmure followed the action of the other two. The trio were now grouped in a standing posture before the fire.

"It is a large question you have proposed, Claverhouse," said Kenmure, gravely, "a question on which it would be presuming to enter upon more than concerns our immediate affairs. The Lochinvars have never been unfaithful to the Crown. If they err, it is more likely to be in carrying their duty to the Crown beyond what is due to the people and the country, and eventually to the Crown itself.

The question to-day is not a question of
loyalty, but a question of ecclesiastical order,
in which that of loyalty to the Crown has
become so unfortunately mixed that priests
and ecclesiastics, with some in their train
from whom better might have been expected,
take upon them to say that all are disloyal
and rebel who do not agree to their precise
ecclesiastical forms.  A soldier and man of
the world like you, Claverhouse, must be
superior to an error of so gross a character.  However, to the practical point of
business before us.  I reclaim strongly
against this hunting to death of every one
concerned or supposed to have been concerned in Bothwell Brig.  It is now an old
story, and should be forgotten, more especially since the Government was victorious.
To extend the harassment to the fathers,
mothers, and relations of the outlaws is
execrable impolicy.  There are the Gordons

of Earlston, Maclellan of Borgue, Bell of
Whiteside, and many others, not impla-
cable or hard to deal with, driven to extremities. A general amnesty should
cover up such sores. We are losing the
chivalrous feeling cherished by our ancestors even in the most barbarous times."

"It is surely necessary," said Claverhouse, " to stop the career of men in arms
or on the eve of taking arms against the
Government. Examples must be made, if
there is to be any terror to evil-doers."

"Examples!" rejoined Kenmure, shaking his head. " For every one you frighten
you make two desperate. Every one even
slain becomes a new tap-root of rebellion.
Men like myself, who would strain every
nerve to repress disorder, are paralyzed.
What good end could be served," added
Kenmure, with a keen glance at Clavers,
" by condemning the old lady of Airioland

to a punishment worse than death itself, and for what? For giving a night's harbour and some bread and cheese to her outlawed son! It is not that she is a kinswoman of mine, for of whatever family it would be the same. But how is the Chief of the Gordons placed when women of his own blood are thus degraded and tortured before his eyes?"

" Her house, my lord, " replied Clavers, " was a haunt of fanatic preachers and armed rebels—an open, daily affront to the authority of the King. The sentence, indeed, was extreme, intendedly extreme, as a warning. But not a hair of the dame has been injured, and she might no doubt be released on the surrender of her son."

" True," said Kenmure. " Yet how obtain the surrender of a wild cat that has lived on the hill-tops so many years? If

he could be induced to banish himself
abroad as a ransom of his mother it would
be a good thing. I should be glad to help
in such an arrangement."

"I fear, my lord," replied Clavers,
"you do not see the whole situation of the
Government. These goings abroad have
had no good result. The Hague is a nest
of rebels and conspirators. Better to have
kept them at home under some control.
But I engage there shall be no haste in the
case of lady Hay, the comfort of the dame
in the meanwhile cared for, and your
interest consulted in other affairs. Yet
let me finally entreat you, my Lord Kenmure, to put your hand to the roll which
now binds in golden loyalty the baronage
of Galloway."

"Do, dear Kenmure," urged the lady,
"do. It is only a form. I am sure they
cannot expect you to do more for the

peace than you have been doing. But it will help Claverhouse to strengthen your interest with the Council. Do, my dear lord," added the lady, as she advanced and leaned upon his shoulder, " do what so many have done."

" Sit down, Grizzel," said Kenmure, " I shall consider of it. What is your route, Captain Graham ? "

Claverhouse replied that his quarters would be at Kirkcuthbert for two or three days.

" I shall meet you there," said Kenmure, holding out his hand; and in a few moments Clavers had taken his place amid an escort of dragoons in front of the Castle, and was riding along the avenue lighted by torch-bearers to the gate.

# CHAPTER VIII.

I had rather have a fool to make me merry, than experience to make me sad.

*As You Like It.*

NEXT morning the soldiers quartered in the burg and the manse were early on horseback at the inn, answering trumpets from the Castle having signalled the preparations of the party there for the march. It had been a night of rain; and heavy clouds, under gusts of cold wind, were still discharging occasional showers. When all was ready, and Clavers descended with his usual light and hurried step to the street, the first object that caught his eye was

Allan Peerie standing before the head of
his charger, smoothing its nostrils, and
looking from side to side with childlike
curiosity at the curve of its neck and the
ornaments of its bridle and martingale.
Clavers suddenly stopped, and taking a
small silver box scarce an inch square from
his pocket sniffed its contents, while he
surveyed with a sense of exquisite drollery
this wild and tattered though familiar
figure.  Stepping forward to the Fool, and
holding out the open box, "Take a pinch,
Peerie," he said, with the most pleasant
sympathy ; " it will warm your blue nose."
Allan dipped his finger into the box,
snuffed, and then sneezed so much as to
give Clavers much pleasure.

"Are you going on the march to-day?"
asked Clavers, clapping Allan on the
shoulder.

The Fool gave a shake of his head, and

added, " I'm cauld, wet, and hungry," his teeth clattering like a pair of castanets.

Allan threw his arms round the neck of the charger while Clavers sprang into the saddle.

" Gordon," he said to the landlord, waiting in front of the hostelry, " take poor Peerie to a fire, and give him a good breakfast. Nay, stop ! Come along with us, Peerie, a little way, and I will introduce you to Kenmure." At a wave of his hand the trumpet sounded, was speedily answered from the Castle, and the troop moved forward, Allan pacing along with the usual pomp by the side of Clavers' gallant steed.

On the party approaching the outer gate of the Castle the troopers stationed there filed out of the avenue, and were followed by Kenmure on horseback, to whom Claverhouse drew up, and after the passing

salutations, said, with a humorous smile,
"May I commend to your hospitality,
my lord, this Sir Fool hanging on my
stirrup? He is in a worse plight this
morning than I have seen him." Kenmure
nodded and laughed at the odd appearance
of Allan. "I shall dispense with his services to-day," added Clavers, as he moved
after his troop, "on condition that he
makes due appearance at Kirkcuthbert."
These last words had probably an oblique
allusion to Kenmure himself. So the
Viscount seemed to take them. "I will
ride down the day after to-morrow," was
his reply.

Kenmure's eye followed the troop till
they had disappeared, when Allan, approaching, handed him a piece of paper,
folded, but not addressed, and tied with a
thread. Thinking it was some petition, he
thrust it into his pocket, and called to the

gatekeeper—" Ho ! Take this poor man down to the butler, and tell him to give him to eat and drink till I return." He then rode into the burg.

At the hostelry the Viscount learned that the five men, whom Claverhouse mildly spoke of the previous evening to Lady Kenmure as having been " apprehended," had in reality been shot, and that their dead bodies were lying unburied on the moor. The names of several of the victims could even be repeated to him. He returned to the Castle moody, horrified, and incensed. What stupidity or hypocrisy, he thought, for Queensberry to talk of preserving the baronial authority, while this tool, Claverhouse, so pleasant and courteous in speech and so reckless and cold-blooded in action, is making us all a hissing and a mockery to the people on our own estates ! Upon entering his private room he thought of the missive he had received from Peerie, and opening it more with a view of diverting the gloomy current of his thoughts than finding any importance in its contents, read as follows :—

"Believe not a word of Clavers' hue-and-cry of assassination. I could have slain the coward, and avenged myself in his heart's blood as easily as ever I struck down a wasp. My sole object was to challenge him to fair combat with our swords, and to surrender myself to his arm if superior to mine.

"This is to notify that I relax of nothing in my purpose. I shall track him from place to place as long as he dares to remain in Galloway, and when it can be done in the presence of witnesses, he must fight me like a man of honour, or die the craven death he deserves.

"As for my mother, of whom the beast

has made a helpless prey, they shall only transport her from her native soil over my dead body. God helping me, I shall carry her out of their pitiless and bloody hands, to the place where, if anywhere on earth, she may claim and must find protection.

"Wm. Hay."

Kenmure, on reading this epistle, was distracted by the most conflicting interpretations and emotions. That it was a true account of the attack on Claverhouse in his head-quarters he had already gathered enough to believe; and it was only what a rational judgment would conceive that a brave and dashing young man like Hay, pursued so many years as an outlaw, and now riven in the tenderest core of his being by the doom that had fallen, mainly on his account, upon his widowed mother, would act and resolve in this daring and relentless spirit. But might the letter, on the other hand, not be a trick of Clavers—an attempt of that wily character to force Kenmure into the net which he had been weaving round him time after time? His ready offer of accommodation in the case of Lady Hay was catching, but it was not explicit, was fenced round with difficult conditions, and might be all too hypocritical in one who had imbrued his hands that afternoon most wantonly in the blood of five men of humble life. There was something unreal, if not bitterly sarcastic, moreover, in his demeanour at the gate. What could mean his silly, if not ostentatious or double-minded, transfer of the Fool to the hospitality of the Castle? Was it one of those passing whims of benevolence by which a seared and conscienceless mortal compounded for much lawless ambition and many cruelties? Was it possible that this wandering idiot could be a favourite of Claverhouse, and yet be a bearer the while of an important letter from his deadly enemy, Hay?

Kenmure summoned the butler.

"What of the vagrant I sent down from the gate?"

"Allan Peerie, my lord? He is in the servants' hall, has been weel enterteened, and been anxious to get awa, but I thocht it necessar to deteen him till your lordship should say."

"Bring him here, and leave us together."

"Dinna be severe, my lord, on Allan. He's a puir feckless cratur, weel kent in the country side, and in his private talk is no ow'r frienly to Clavers—but an honest cratur nevertheless, scarcely kens sometimes, I believe, what he says."

"Begone, sir, and do as I have ordered,"

K 2

said Kenmure, in a torment of dis-
quietude.

When Allan was closeted with Lord
Kenmure he bore all the appearance of a
vagrant crackbrain of the time.

" You delivered to me this writing ? "
Allan nodded assent.

" It is a writing, of course, from Claverhouse, I see—a message he had not time
to deliver verbally, and left with you to
deliver as a kindly warrant on the hospitality of the Castle. It is like my gay and
gallant friend Clavers."

Allan, by every fool-like expression of
voice and gesture, decidedly negatived this
origin of the document.

" No," said Kenmure. " Who, then, is
the writer ? Who gave it you ? To whom
were you to deliver it ? Where did you
get it ? To whom are you to take an answer ?" To all which rapid interrogations

Allan signified his inability to give any intelligible reply.

"You must not juggle with me, varlet," said Kenmure, rising to his feet sternly. "This paper is either from Claverhouse, or to me from some one else. Answer, or I shall send you instantly to the dungeon of the Castle."

"I am neither answerable to Clavers," replied Allan, throwing off his fool-like demeanour, and instead of a vacant and wandering gaze, fixing his eyes steadily on Kenmure, "nor to you, my lord, but to a higher Power. It is an honest paper, honestly delivered. But I can neither tell you whence it came nor whither it goeth. It must speak for itself."

Kenmure sat down as if to read the missive, and as he peered upward more than once from the paper his eyes were met by the calm and intelligent gaze of Allan.

" It is signed Wm. Hay," said the Viscount.   " You know Hay ?"

" I know him," replied Allan.

" Then tell him from me that he must be
peaceable and wary—that I am endeavour-
ing more than he can hope to accomplish
by any lawless or desperate courses of his—
and that I shall see him face to face in fair
honour if he should wish.   That is my reply to what you have brought.   You may
leave."

Claverhouse, in his martial progress to
Kircuthbert, observed the usual tactics.
He sent out flanking parties to the farm-
houses, and sweeping a breadth of country
after passing from the narrow shore of Loch
Ken, had the sport of driving four men into
a deep and brambly loop of the Dee, within
view of the sombre walls of Threave Castle.
Two of the men, armed with fowling-pieces,
when pressed by a party of dismounted

troopers, started from their lair, and would have taken the river, but were arrested by several pistol shots, under which they fell wounded. The other two, unarmed, were seized, and dragged from the bushes into the presence of Claverhouse. They said they had gone out to shoot teal and wild ducks in the lakelets and marshes, through which the waters of the Ken and Dee pass into a common river. The wounded men, when brought forward, gave the same account. Then followed the usual questions. Had they been tested? No. Then they must take the Test now, and find sureties for their good behaviour; but they declined with rueful looks, as if unable to comply, rather than making any verbal answer.

"Finish the work on these wounded rogues who have dared to carry arms against the King," cried Clavers; and a platoon of musketeers in a few moments had stretched them lifeless where they stood in the pain and blood of their previous wounds.

The other two were bound, and carried into Kircuthbert, where a hasty court-martial was held the following morning—Clavers and Lagg presiding — and the prisoners condemned to immediate execution on the gallows for being out in an armed party, refusing the Test, and for rebellion, as set out in a sentence covering the case of their companions, " fatally wounded in their temerity on the field."

# CHAPTER IX.

Here's Kenmure's health in wine, Willie!
    Here's Kenmure's health in wine;
There ne'er was a coward o' Kenmure's blude,
    Nor yet o' Gordon's line.

*Burns.*

WHEN Kenmure rose from an uneasy couch on the day of his engagement to meet Claverhouse at Kircuthbert, it was not to debate whether he should hold the promised parley. The agony of irresolution was over. In the ferment of his mind the last two days he had passed from one extreme to another. He would place his castle in a state of defence, assemble his retainers around him, exercise jurisdiction

on his own lands at least, resisting all
acts of ferocious tyranny over his tenants
and dependents, and holding with single-
minded loyalty and bravery what still
belonged to him as a peer of Scotland and
a baron of Galloway. This would be better
than tamely to allow himself to be bereft
piecemeal of every legal right, and to be
reduced to a mere cypher in his own
stronghold. Then the thought occurred to
him that this resolution, however worthy
and excellent, might now be too late;
he had been stripped of the bailiary of
Tongueland and other official functions;
his influence as a lord and magistrate was
already much diminished; all the local juris-
dictions were suppressed, or in abeyance
to this devouring Sheriffship of the
Grahams; his most powerful friends had
succumbed one after another, or been
ruthlessly dispossessed under the dominant

tyranny; and the common men, whose stout thews and sinews would have been a wall of defence round the native magistracy of Galloway, were being daily swept down by the dragonnades of Clavers. In this vacillating frame of mind, however, Kenmure put away from him indignantly all further submission in the meanwhile to the purposes and proceedings of the Government, as represented by Claverhouse. He would go to Kircuthbert, but he would go to complain and remonstrate, not to equivocate or to yield; he would be a drag on this fiery wheel till such time as he could lay an appeal before the Council at Edinburgh or the King at Whitehall. He fancied he saw in the suave and persevering arts with which Claverhouse had plied him a proof that he still enjoyed some freedom of counsel.

Kenmure accordingly set out early to

Kircuthbert, with more state than usual
in a simple ride to the chief town of the
Stewartry, every mile of which had long
been as free and secure as a royal road to
the House of Lochinvar.   In addition to
his sword he had pistols in his belt, and
pistols in his holsters, and was attended by
six mounted retainers sufficiently armed.

On approaching the town he perceived
that two dragoons were posted at the
entrance to the High Street, and that the
old gate, swung round on its rusty hinges,
was closed, while a number of country
people, refused admittance, stood at a little
distance, or were wandering about seeking some other inlet to the town.   The
dragoons saluted Kenmure, and, the gate
opening, he and his attendants passed
through.   The High Street was alive with
people.   It seemed as if men, women, and
children were all out of doors.   The crowd

was dense in front of the gaol, where two
dead bodies were hanging in chains from
a gibbet erected over the market cross,
with dragoons moving round the place of
execution amid occasional jeers and hissings
from a portion of the mob.

Kenmure turned his horse's head towards
the Castle, where he was informed by the
sentries that Claverhouse had left the previous afternoon, taking most of the force
along with him, but was to return in course
of the day. "When were these men put
to death?" he inquired. "Yesterday forenoon," was the reply. "The cause of the
commotion is the long exposure of the
bodies," observed Kenmure, and on learning the name of the officer in command of
the guard at the gaol, was proceeding in
that direction when he was met by the
Provost and the Sheriff-clerk, both in a
state of agitation.

They were afraid of a collision between the troopers and the populace.

"Take down the bodies for decent burial," said Kenmure, "and order the people to retire to their houses."

"The lord-sheriff, my lord," said the Provost, "has left no direct order as to the disposal of the bodies." The chief magistrate, afraid of the people and no less afraid of Claverhouse, was trembling between the horns of a dilemma, either of which was dreadful to his imagination.

"The Sheriff cannot be offended at what is needful to keep the King's peace within the bounds of the regality," observed Kenmure. "Have the bodies removed at once. I will stand between you and Claverhouse for so much."

"My Lord Kenmure," interposed the Sheriff-clerk, "I think you advise wisely.

But you will accompany us to the Cross ? "

" It is there I am going," said the Viscount.

A total hush ensued among the crowd in the High Street as Kenmure advanced with the Provost on one side and the Sheriff-clerk on the other, followed by his men-at-arms. Not a word of reproach was hurled at the Provost, and the small party of dragoons was left in undisturbed possession of the gallows and its lifeless prey.

"Let the Magistrates remove the bodies," said Kenmure, addressing the military officer, " and this turmoil will cease."

" Bodies ! " said the somewhat truculent Sergeant-major, who had obviously been fortifying his ghastly and weary duty by liberal potations. " Is it thae things ye ca' bodies, my lord ? They're naething but scaurcraws. Gude faith, it's no the custom o' oor service to part wi' oor scaurcraws as lang as they'll keep. Damn it, I wad like to see wha wad daur to touch them."

"That may be," whispered Kenmure. "But we are not very strong here at present. It is not the burgesses alone; the country is rising in our rear. There is a large gathering outside the north gate."

"Weel, if there be ony danger, my Lord Kenmure, and if ye are ready to tak our noble high Captain on your ain head, the magistrates may do what they like wi' the bodies for me. But martial law is law martial, my lord, ye ken as I do, and they maun be ready to produce them and hang them up again if our noble high Captain should demand it. That's the only safety I can see for any saul amang us. The Provost and us hae been bickering aboot it a' day without seeing ony way oot o' the wood."

The bodies were taken down from the gibbet, and Kenmure finding the troopers sufficiently under his control in the absence of their Captain, returned to the Castle to wait his arrival.

Clavers, accompanied by Lagg, had gone into the neighbouring parish of Borgue. He had never visited Galloway without this ceremony to Borgue. The reason of such devoted attention is curious, but distinctly symptomatic of an inveterate disease in the blood of the Scotch Administration at this ill-fated period. Maclellan of Barmagechan, a gentleman of property and influence in the parish, had been at the battle of Bothwell Brig, and been outlawed and severely harried in his substance, like many others, for that unforgettable rebellion. The lapse of years

had no power of quenching the fury of the
Royalist faction against every person of
mark in the country known or suspected
to have engaged in a fight, with the immediate result of which none had so much
reason to be satisfied as the faction themselves. Their inexhaustible vengeance was
extended to the relations and private
friends of the outlaws, regardless of whatever social dislocation might ensue. Maclellan had at length been seized and
banished to the Plantations. But this
example, severe as it was, failed to shake
the stout-hearted resolution of the people
of Borgue, who remained in all their
original alienation from the Curate and the
fiery policy of the Privy Council. The
object of Claverhouse's visits was to disarm
and terrorize the parish, rich in substance
as it was sturdy in political and religious
independence, and all the more valuable as

a prey, while dangerous as an enemy or support of enemies.

In the interval of Clavers' return on this occasion to the head town, Kenmure had opportunity of learning from the local officials, who gathered around him in the Castle, the circumstances of the hanging of the two men, with the still more summary execution of their companions on the spot where they were taken; and, what probably horrified him as much, that Bell of Whiteside some days before had been shot in his own fields by Lagg, who had interdicted the burial of the dead body. These revelations roused the nerve of Kenmure, and prepared what was destined to be a stormy scene.

On Clavers and Lagg arriving before the burghal castle, surrounded by a large military escort, Kenmure opened the upper window where he was seated, in welcome to the party, and by this movement probably averted an ebullition outside. Claverhouse was already calling in a peremptory tone for the Sergeant-major of the guard, and loud voices were heard in the vestibule and on the staircase as he ascended.

"It is all a d—d deal too quiet for me," Lagg was saying to Clavers, as they entered the apartment where Kenmure stood to receive them. "To remove the gallows-birds before they were a day auld, and in a nest of rotten Whugs too, where they would have been so usefu'—it's hell on earth, perfect hell on earth."

"Sheriff," said Kenmure, "what has been done is well done. But if there is anything wrong do not blame any of your officers, or any of the magistrates. I alone am to blame. The town was in a state of disorder when I entered, and I advised the removal of the bodies, to which all agreed. That is what has occurred with no unhappy results."

" My lord," replied Claverhouse, " I have no doubt your advice was of good intention, but I can ill brook to have my authority snperseded where you have no authority whatever."

" It was the testimony of all," rejoined Kenmure, " that you had given no express order as to the disposal of the bodies, and you will surely not contend, order or no order, that on such a matter the King's peace should be disturbed in one of his royal burghs."

" Kenmure and the King's peace !" cried Lagg, with an insulting laugh.

" My friend and relative," said Kenmure, quivering with excitement, but still in temper, "you are the last man to take the King's name into your mouth. What have you done? What are your hands red and filthy with at this moment? Without form of law or authority you have slain Bell of Whiteside; a gentleman bred and born, an unoffending subject and neighbour, as the whole country side will testify; and you have had the barbarism to threaten with your vengeance any one who dares to lift his dead body. You have dishonoured the King whom you pretend to serve; you have dishonoured the name of gentleman."

" Curse on the souls of a' sic gentlemen," roared Lagg. " As for the body, Kenmure, tak it up, man, if you will; tak it, and put it in your beef-tub."

Kenmure could bear no more. He drew his sword, and would have run it through the body of Lagg, but for the intervention of Claverhouse, who rushed between the two. " Silence, Grierson! Your ill-scraped tongue, as I have told you more than once, is enough to upset the monarchy! Forbear, my lord! Do not bring scandal on yourself and us by a brawl with your kinsman.

"Kinsman! unworthy!" Kenmure sneered, as he returned his sword to the sheath.

This was the worst possible introduction to the business on which Claverhouse was intent with the master of Kenmure Castle; and when, on having dismissed Lagg on some garrison and stable duties, he would have entered on a more politic course, Kenmure rose and said, "I shall enter into no further treaty till I have reported these proceedings to the Council, and, failing that, to Whitehall!"

"Do nothing hasty, my lord," said Claverhouse in a haughty tone, as he followed Kenmure a few steps towards the door. "You will find at the Council that I have not exceeded my commission. Stair and his glib-tongued son have tried that game, and you know what has come of it."

It was dark before Kenmure and his men reached the Boat of Rhone at the confluence of the Ken and the Dee, where a pontoon of semi-military structure, after the fashion on the French and other continental rivers, afforded a passage for cattle and vehicles. But the moon had now risen, and was gleaming brightly over the broad pools of the lagoon and the deep waters of Loch Ken as the party approached the boat bridge. While the retainers were placing their horses on the raft, Kenmure looked up the lake towards the Castle, and, the moonlit scene being so calm and tranquillizing, was hesitating whether to take a skiff, and go home the rest of the way by water, when a muffled figure rose at a little distance and approached him. It was William Hay. Kenmure, on the recognition, dismounted, and walked aside with this unexpected companion.

The outlaw of Arioland poured out his spirit in full measure to Kenmure in this interview, as he thought, the last he was likely to have with any of the barons of Galloway. Hope of public resistance to the tyranny, he confessed in a tone more of sorrow than of anger, had well-nigh died within him. He recounted all the marks of cowardice and backsliding with a depth of dejection, as if measuring out the total loss and ruin of the country, mingled with a personal courage of despair, which startled Kenmure all the more that in both chords it found some echoes in his own breast. "The public cause is lost," said Hay. "You will all have to bow your necks, and will scarcely save your lives under the yoke.

But I have a private cause which is not lost. And of which I do not despair. I shall rescue my mother or die in the attempt."

Kenmure, while admitting the prostrate and tragic situation of which his own mind was full enough, reminded Hay that any public armed resistance would encounter the whole force not only of the Scotch, but the English Government, and that there was some plea, though probably not wholly valid, for the diplomacy of self-preservation so generally adopted. "I do not know," said Kenmure, "whether I can preserve myself or not, but I have not been forgetful either of the public interest or the safety of my private friends. I have spoken so strongly to Claverhouse of the iniquity of the sentence on your mother that he has said it may be cancelled on conditions. Of these conditions I cannot speak to you freely, because I myself do not see my way through them."

" Conditions !" said Hay eagerly. " Why hesitate ? Save my mother, Kenmure, and do anything you please with me. Quarter me, chip me into pieces, or burn me alive, and scatter my ashes to the four winds of heaven, if you save my mother ! "

" Yes," said Kenmure, " but it is difficult to see how the two ends are to meet. It would be easy to dispose of you in your present mood. Tie a stone round your neck, for instance, and throw you into Loch Ken. But your mother ? Clavers says your absolute surrender. I say your conditional but voluntary removal from the country—"

" Say no more, my lord," interrupted Hay, " I would not trust a lock of my hair on the word of Clavers or any of his faction. They would shoot, hang, or drown you, me, anybody the one moment, and forget the condition of it all the next. But let my mother be freed and secure, and I am willing to leave the country never to return. All I love now on earth I shall then be able to protect. But I shall never surrender, my lord, never. Farewell!" And Hay, parting thus from Kenmure, leaped into a boat on the Lochside; and as Kenmure looked, the boat under two stout rowers was darting swiftly over the waters.

# CHAPTER X.

1. But is this law ?
2. Ay, marry is't; crowner's 'quest law.
Clowns in Hamlet.

WE must now return to Glenvernoch, where
we left the farmer under summons to appear
before the Sheriff-depute the day after
Claverhouse's flaming despatch announcing
his attempted assassination by Hay.　This
summons Glenvernoch duly obeyed; and he
set out with a stout heart, amid the cruel
anxieties of his wife and daughters, on a
journey to the county town, which he had
so often sadly to repeat in the course of the
next four months, that the slightest fore-

cast of what was to happen would probably
have dashed his bravery of spirit on this
first occasion.   Glenvernoch held the legal
faculty in the lowest possible repute.   " A
summons to appear," served by any but a
baron-bailie, or for any other purpose than
the payment of his land dues, was, in Glenvernoch's eyes, an utter abomination, re-
flecting only disgrace on all parties concerned, from the judge downward.   There
was a smell about a court-house and gaol to
his nostrils, and thence infecting the whole
legal fraternity, to which that of a " braxy"
itself was like the perfume of roses.   But
conscious rectitude of purpose enabled Glenvernoch to meet this summons with a light
heart, and the unconcealed distress of his
family only drew out his own spirit.   " Hoot-
toot, woman," he said to his wife, as she
busied round him, and wailed her doubts
and fears, " what can the Sherra-depo want

o' me but advice? Puir stranger chiel, he's nae doot in mickle need o' some sense."

"It may be mair serious than ye dreed, faither," said Margaret, in her more solemn and tenderly-imperious way. "If ye say a wrang word, they may twist it aboot their ain gate and gie us a' much grief."

"But I'll no say a wrang word, Maggie, wean. I'll tell the truth, and if the truth be wrang it will no be your faut or mine, my bonnie queen."

"Corporal M'Graw," said the farmer to the officer in charge of the party of soldiers at Glenvernoch, and who had been a witness of these family confidences, "keep your red-coats weel in haun', my man, while I'm doon at the Shirra. There's aye much usefu' wark aboot a farm toon. The middens are getting clean ow'r big. We begin aboot this time o' the year to carry oot the fulzie to the infields before the pleughin'. Sandy will hae the hurdles a' ready.  The fallows couldna hae better exercise, and they can aye hae a spell at the fishing when inclined. But without a clud in the sky and a bit spate in the burn the fishing is idle wark, Corporal M'Graw—a mere walloping o' the water to nae purpose."

The bold and ingenious spirit of the farmer, when he entered appearance in Sheriff Graham's Court half an hour inside the date of summons, somewhat disconcerted that dignitary.  In point of fact, the Sheriff-depute scarce expected an appearance at all till it should be secured by apprehension and military force.  But, with the help of the clerk, he had been drawing out a narrative to be transformed into an indictment, on which any measure, penalty, or sentence might be endorsed at will.  It was a procedure in *foro clauso*, but it was likely to become clamorous enough when Glenvernoch, after sitting quietly in the little Court-room till his patience was exhausted, rose and asked of the scriveners, ushers, and other fleeting shadows of the place, "Whar's the Sherra? Sherra-depo' Graham—that's to say, whar's he? Bring the Sherra-depo' afore me, or I'll gang awa' hame again."

This uproar of Glenvernoch had to be conveyed to the Sheriff-depute, and when that functionary appeared with the clerk, and took his seat, the farmer advanced to the bar, and holding out the summons, said, "That's what has brocht me here, please your honour."

"You are Gilbert Wilson, farmer, Glenvernoch," said the Sheriff-depute? "I am," said the farmer. "May I ask, are ye the Sherra-depo'?" to which question Mr. Graham, tickled by a demeanour wholly new to him, returned a decided smile of assent. "I'm glad o' that, your honour, added the farmer; " what hae ye, then, to say to me ? "

" Seat yourself, Glenvernoch," said the Sheriff-depute, " and you will hear. Clerk, read the process."

The paper read to Glenvernoch, after the manner of a *procès-verbal* in the French criminal courts, narrated all the circumstances of the official information already known to the reader, heightening the gravity and darkening the colour of each as the development of the crime of assassination proceeded from its first inception to its climax, and piecing the various incidents so artfully as to form a chain of circumstantial evidence that the plot must have been hatched on the farm of Glenvernoch, with full knowledge and assent of the people thereon. As the story advanced into the horror of the attempt itself, the crafty and cold-blooded procedure of

the assassin, the ferocity with which he
attempted to pistol and stab to death the
King's lieutenant in Galloway, and how
nearly the villain was of accomplishing his
malignant, bloody, and hellish purpose, the
farmer became more deeply interested in
this startling narrative of news, only a day
or two old, than any one would now be in
reading a similar tale in the morning news-
papers or the *Police Gazette*.    What with
absorption in the main recital, and anguish
at the pathetic situation of Claverhouse,
the farmer, towards the close of the reading, wholly lost sight of the underlying
threads of insinuation that he himself was
a party in the tragedy.

"It's a dreedfu' business," said Glenvernoch, half choking with emotion. "Actually
horrible, as I should say sae, Sherra. What
can hae possessed the mad cratur, think ye,
to tak' sic a loup in the dark ? Is there ony

advice I can gie you, Sherra, in what must
be to you sic painfu' circumstances—mair
sae as Claverhouse is your ain brither?
I'm sure I sympatheeze wi' you deeply,
Sherra, in this mad-like business."

"I am afraid," said the Sheriff-depute,
in a tone of freezing sarcasm, " that you
misunderstand the process, my good man.
You have been summoned here as act and
part with William Hay in this monstrous
crime."

Ready as Glenvernoch was to enter into
the griefs and anxieties of the Graham
family, as set forth in the *procès-verbal*, to
this pointed suggestion of his own concern
in the matter he was no less ready to
respond, and, rising to his feet, manfully
delivered himself of such a massy array of
ingenuous denial, protest, and defiance as
completely shook the self-possession of the
Sheriff-depute.   "Me—airt and pairt—wi'

Wully Hay—in assassination!" spake Glenvernoch through his teeth, with a disdain
of voice and expression that might have
ground a mountain into dust. " I never
spak three words wi' the assassin in my life.
Naething to me your proceeds or rigma-
roles. Bring the man afore me that will
say the contrar' to what I say."

" It cannot be disputed, Glenvernoch,"
said the Sheriff-depute, " that Hay was
last seen, before his great crime, on your
farm, that he was in company with mistress
Martha Dunbar and your daughter Margaret, and that he was in arms—the arms
by which, it would appear, he made this
murderous attempt."

" And what if a' that should be true,
Sherra," replied the farmer, " am I or my
dochter to be answerable for ony strangers
that may come on the farm, and for what
they may exploit, the dare-deils, thretty

miles awa'? It's no common sense. As
for lady Martha, I understood she was under freedom o' the Government as long as
she was clear o' friskies in the Machars,
and I'm much misteen if ye dinna fin' that
oot. The young woman was as quate as a
lamb in my hoose."

Mr. Depute Graham, after some delibera-
tion with himself, in which he reclined
almost horizontally on his chair, and his
eyes, though closed, seemed directed to the
highest point of the ceiling, at length
raising himself, and addressing the clerk
rather than Glenvernoch, said, " I wad fain
believe Gilbert Wilson to be an honest and
loyal man."

" Na, dinna say fain, Sherra," inter-
pleaded Glenvernoch, " but just say honest
and loyal man outricht, until proved to be
otherwise—"

" Yes, Glenvernoch," said the Sheriff-depute, further rousing himself, " but the circumstances are so suspicious, and the case itself so important, that the least I can adjudge to-day is that a sufficient body of soldiers be quartered on the farm, and that you give a new bond of 500 merks for your good behaviour, paying up the old."

" As for my gude behaviour, honestly interprat," replied Glenvernoch, " I'll gie you my bond for a thoosand merks, sir, but this quartering o' sogers is a mair particular matter, and needs to be properly understood. If it gangs ow'r far I had better gie ye the farm to yoursells."

Glenvernoch had a long contest with the Sheriff-depute and the Clerk as to the number to be quartered, the rations for each man, what they were to have for breakfast, dinner, and supper, and how and where they were to be bedded. These points were finally arranged with some diffi-

culty—the number of men fixed at ten in
the meanwhile, to be fed in the ordinary
custom of the farm-house; but no salmon,
or white, or burn trout at any of the diets
oftener than twice-a-week—the men to
sleep in the outhouses, with such decent
and ample accommodation as the farmer
could afford; but Corporal M'Graw and
such superior officers as might visit Glenvernoch to have the best beds in the farm-
house. The Sheriff-depute, having yielded
on several points, finally insisted that occasional parties of cavalry coming and going
through Glenvernoch should have refreshment for man and horse, with all hospitable
treatment and furtherance in their mission,
and that the present decree should in no
sense be deemed an *ultimatum;* to which
the farmer objected as being terms of sentence "withoot boonds, and consequently
beyond a' human obligation." But the

Sheriff-depute was peremptory, and Glenvernoch, with a final protest that "the
sentence micht last a wee while, but couldna
last lang," signed the personal caution for
500 merks, and was allowed to leave the
obnoxious smell of the Court room—ruffled
in temper, and down in the mouth, but
with the sense of freedom of a man, who,
having fought a stout battle, has escaped
with his life, and with some remaining
control over his means of subsistence.

The first person Glenvernoch met on the
Court-room stair was his cattle-dealing ac-
quaintance Picardy, who was exuberantly
friendly in his congratulations.

"I am so glad ye hae got aff, Glen—got
aff glorious, Glen? Hang me, it's what I
hae always said; Glenvernoch never can
be beat. Let me shake your hand, Glen;
ye've come aff sae bravely."

"Taut," said Glenvernoch, with no apparent disposition to shake hands. "I kenna, Tam, what ye mean by aff and on here. To me it seems a' maistly fwables. But your new Sherra-depo' is a gey yaul chiel. He kens as weel as ony hoo to mak' a brick oot o' a strae. But that's naething to the purpose, Tam. Whan are ye to settle your wayleave through the farm? It is lickly to prove a costly affair to me."

"I'm to be up the country the incoming week, and will look in and settle handsomely," Picardy assured the farmer. "But I maun see ye aff, Glen. Whaur dae ye pit up?"

"The pownie's in Lucky Carnochan's at the Craig," replied the farmer; and they went together to the inn, where, in the interval of bringing out Glenvernoch's horse, the drover over a hasty dram roundly cursed Hay as the cause of mischief and ruin to every one connected with him.

"But the rope is weel roon his neck noo," he added, "and it behoves us a' to gie the rascal a wide berth and a short shrift for the future."

"Gude e'en, Tam," observed the farmer as he rode off, "but mind the settlement, man.   It canna be postpooned a day langer than ye hae said."

# CHAPTER XI.

So nicely balanced are true sympathies,
That a grain in one scale turns the other.
*Fragment.*

GLENVERNOCH, as the stir of contention in
the Court-room gave place to reflection on
what had occurred, became more heavy in
spirit every mile of the road to his farm
steading. He could not conceal from himself that he was no longer the master he
had been over his own affairs; that he
had no longer the laird of Castle-
Stewart only to deal with under the
customary dues of a baronial holding,
nor could even depend on the laird as a

defender against any wrong done to him. He felt keenly that a harpy had now entered upon his farm, superior to all power or right therewith connected that might soon disembowel it of its substance—stock, lock, and barrel. While he had his own doubt of the truth of the charge against Hay, and a full share of belief in the possible capacity of Claverhouse for lying to serve his own ends, yet he reasoned that if the heads of the law said there was an attempted assassination, the saying would be as deadly for all practical purposes as if it were a fact. The encounter between Hay and Picardy at the head of the glen he had looked upon as a mere brawl, of which young women might have happened to become witnesses, and which they had probably interrupted. That they were the cause of such an event, or could be parties to it in any sense, was dismissed by Glenvernoch as unworthy of conjecture. It was clear from the conduct of Picardy that he did not consider himself injured on that occasion either by Glenvernoch or his daughter. That an affair of this kind should be criminally connected with an attempted murder at so great a distance as Newton-Galloway was beyond the comprehension of the farmer; but the overbearing power of the law, when impelled on a given track, was comprehensible to him enough under all the events of the late years; and as he rode moodily through the "yett" to the farm-house, with ten red coats and a corporal in possession, and sentries walking their rounds, he felt like one under the glaring eyes and open jaws of a monster, whose fangs were already fastening round all that was dear to him on earth.

Glenvernoch's wife and daughters had

passed a day of such anxious forebodings
lest he might be cast into prison, or
detained on some pretext or other of the
Sheriff-depute, that they heard his voice
calling upon Sandy with a sense of relief,
and gathered round him in the fondest
welcome. But the more cheerful and smil-
ing Glenvernoch saw his family to be, as he
sat down among them, the more sadly the
gloomy thoughts to which he had been
yielding weighed on his own spirit. He
recited to them baldly the burdens and
conditions that had been imposed upon
him, the difficulty he had had in obtaining
alleviations of the decree ready to be
passed, and expressed his fears that this
was but the beginning of worse op-
pressions.

The matron, in her usual calm and hope-
ful spirit, endeavoured to throw some rays
of light over the future. " In my opinion

it will sune blaw ower," she said; "and as for the sojers, we needna forefecht oorsels aboot them. We hae aften as mony folk at the thrang times as we are like to hae a week or twa in the dead o' the year."

Margaret, who had been mostly silent, was suffering under all her serenity of aspect much agony of spirit as she listened to her father. Since the quartering of the soldiers a trail of pollution had seemed to her to have passed over the homestead, and now when she learned that the quartering was to last for an indefinite period, and might any day be increased and rendered more rude and noisome, her abhorrence was intensified. It was not only the wounded pride of a maiden, born and bred in the independence of the hill farms, on seeing her father in the grips of the law and overborne in his own house, that lacerated the heart of Margaret, though of this feeling she had a peculiarly sensitive experience. The sense of humiliation when bailiffs sit down and make themselves free and insolent for the payment of debt, or the foul infection which seems to sully every part of one's house, on discovering that burglars have been through it during the night, have carried away many heirlooms, fumbled among one's letters, and rifled many private repositories, would be but a faint image of the situation as it now presented itself to our heroine. For Margaret, in her religious imagination, had hitherto looked on Glenvernoch as a sanctuary where she could hope to preserve a free and pure conscience; and now she saw not only her father humbled, and weak it might be as a reed amid his own substance, and all her household gods in the dust, but the altar she had been so devoutly raising to the One Only trampled upon, and all but thrown down. How she might be able to act and conduct herself in such circumstances filled her with a sense of weakness and forsakenness so new and overpowering that shame and dismay for the first time seemed to course with unbridled fury through her soul.

Since the instalment of Corporal M'Graw and his guard family worship had been discontinued in Glenvernoch. Margaret rose early from the side of her father and mother, and taking Agnes with her retired to their bed-room, where on bended knees she prayed for Divine strength and guidance, that the wicked might be restrained and the pure and upright strengthened, that her own heart might be purified, that she might be kept void of offence even towards her enemies, and enabled to bear her cross nobly but meekly after the example of her Lord and Saviour.

It was probably in the spirit of this petition, and under deep sense of a new crisis in her life, that Margaret did not go to the meeting of the hill-folk at the Caldons on the following Sabbath-day, but shut herself up several hours in the garret chamber. And it was probably with little difference of motive and feeling that Glenvernoch resolved to give an attendance at the Parish Church. He sought to avoid offence to his enemies, but was willing to go further to that end than his daughter would have gone; and it was his thought that in going abroad, and showing himself among those faithful to the authorities, he might, while no insincere worshipper of the Divine Being, be doing something to weaken the arm of power to injure him or his.

## CHAPTER XII.

Base neuters, in their middle way of steering,
Are neither fish, flesh, fowl, nor good red herring:
Nor whigs, nor tories they; nor this, nor that;
Nor birds, nor beasts; but just a kind of bat:
A twilight animal; true to neither cause,
With whiggish wings, but tory teeth and claws.

*Drydiana.*

PICARDY was true to his promise, and Glenvernoch had early notice, on the day of the
"incoming week" appointed, that the drover was riding up, attended by his urchin,
in one of his jolliest moods. His voice,
indeed, was heard some time before his
person was visible from the farm-house,
and had passed over a variety of lilts, as he

wound his way through the heugh, from
"Cock Your Beaver" to "Cauld Kail in
Aberdeen." In passing the sentries at the
"yett" he struck up a stave in honour of
"The Life of a Soldier," and by the time
he arrived at the farm-house seemed
effervescing with jollity and good feeling
through every feature of his face and
every movement of his strong and active
figure.

"Hoo's a' wi' you, Glenvernoch?" he
cried. "Hoo's a' wi' you? I hope I
see you brawly as I'm mysel'," shaking
the farmer's hand with a really cordial
swing.

"No sae bad, no sae bad at a'," replied
Glenvernoch, with less enthusiasm. "But
what's the news, Tam? what's the news,
man?"

"Things are getting brisker, Glen, brisker
every day," affirmed the drover. "Beasts

are in better demand, and prices—wha wad hae thocht it ten days syne?—actually looking up."

"Oo, ay!" said Glenvernoch, with a peculiar prolongation of these short syllables. "Ye'll be wanting to sell me, nae doot. But the news o' the coonty toon, Tam? the law news? We've little else to think aboot noo but the law. Has Clavers come back frae the Glenken, syne?"

"Whish!" whispered Picardy, with an amusing air of mutual confidence. "Tell nae tales oot o' schule, ye ken. But what are we talking here for?" raising his voice loudly. "Let us gang indoor. Words mak' nae bargains. I'm loaded wi' siller, Glen; loaded wi' siller, as Jamie o' the Cocked Beaver, wha had gowd ahint and gowd afore, and silk in every saddle bore."

"Come awa, then," rejoined the farmer;

" but whar's your wullicat boy, Tam ? I haena seen the clever cratur at your tail sin ye cam to the slap."

" He's on afore me," said Picardy. " I hae business farther up the day, and maun mak' a' speed."

Glenvernoch conducted the drover into the private parlour, in consideration of the account to be settled, as well as of the obvious intention of his guest not to talk too freely on public affairs in a farm-house under military guard. The farmer was desirous to learn all that his guest should be willing to communicate of his own free motion or in reply to questions put. The presence of the goodwife was no bar to this arrangement in the opinion of the farmer, nor was it unpleasing to Picardy, who knew well the oneness of husband and wife in this case, and the importance of enlisting the favourable opinions of the chief members of a family. There was one of the number, indeed, whom he rather particularly desired to see every act and to hear every word he meant to do or say on this occasion.

The passage of the drove through the farm was soon disposed of. Picardy's reckoning of the number of head and the dues rather exceeded than fell short of the expectations of the farmer, who honestly admitted that no special damage had been done, " beyond thae awkward events, Tam, of whilk ye ken mair than I ken, tho' bringing me into trouble the end whereof is as impossible to see as the end o' a ravelled reel."

" All I can say," remarked Picardy, " I will answer to you for my doings in that affair, and as for you and your family, Glen, I hae naething but gude to depone. Except for Hay's infernal attempt on the life o' the Sherra-principal nae trouble wad hae come o't whatever, and the case when sifted will clear up itsel'. There's licht afore us a' yet, Glen, I hope. Sae dinna look at the dark side only, like a hoolet at midnicht. Claverhouse, as ye were asking, has returned frae his rides in the Stewartry. There is some talk of his leaving Galloway for somewhar the Government hae mair need o' him; and I'm sure if it were God's wull and his I should be the last to say nay, for it maun be allowed whan on his high horse here he does stir up unco burlies. But why fash oor heads about kirks and politics, Glen, when ony fair and honest dealing may be dune. I really want some of your nowt the day, and I wad raither hae yours than onyane's. Na, dinna laugh at that observe, for deil tak' me but I wad, Glen. There's mair o' the native blacks among them than is common, and when ye offer three or four year aulds for the market,

they're marketable, that they are—nane o'
the skinky half-hunger'd bane-alls o' the
best bluid, to hear the talk, yet the
bluid sae sma' in quantity as to pu'
doon the quality. Ye ken what I mean,
Glen! Ha, ha, ha! Weel ye ken what I
mean!"

Picardy here broke into a roar of laughter, in which Glenvernoch, rubbing his
hands with some glee, joined heartily
enough. Picardy here touched what was
one of the farmer's strongest convictions
in stock-rearing.

"I'm gled to hear ye speakin' that gate,
Tam," said Glenvernoch, "mair especially
on the public affairs, for when a decent,
inoffensive man like me, tho' I say it mysel',
attending tae his business, is hauled before
the Coort, and left barely in his ain lickness,
it doesna look weel—doesna look weel,
man, ava—for the kintra in general. As

for the nowt, Tam, I'se sell ye, gif we can agree sae far as a luckpenny, aff or on."

"They maun be the best black nowt, Glen," urged the drover, "a' o' gude quality, though maybe no a' aqual. I dinna want to rin a riddle through the stock, but simply a' fair shapely beests in bane, and nane ill-clad in flesh; sic cattle as folk in seeing them gang by would say at yince, 'Thae are Glenvernoch nowt!' Gie me that, Glen," added the drover, in one of his frankest and most rollicking airs, " and I'll gie ye ony price, man, ye like to ask within the boonds o' raison and common sense, and mair than that, I'll pay ye doon on the nail. Plenty o' siller! mair than I care to carry wi' me through the muirs—and wad rather as no leave a feck o't in your hauns, Glenvernoch, wi' gude stock ahint me."

"Faither," said Thomas, who, in the family privilege of entry, had come into the parlour, "I'll rin ower and drive in the nowt."

"Ah! Tammas, ma boy," said the farmer, "thou distna ken what a gleg ee oor freen Picardy has for the best. I maun dae that wark mysel'. But ga' oot and fin' Sandy, and tell him I'll need him by-and-by."

"Ye maun bide awee," continued the farmer, "gif we're to deal, Tam. Feint a clute's on the infield. But bide awee, and ye'll hae a fair sample."

"Ye'll stay and tak' your denner, Mr. Picardy," said the goodwife, who, with the help of Agnes, had already begun to lay the table. "What's a' the hurry?"

The drover appeared to adjust himself easily to this arrangement, and, in company

with Glenvernoch and Mrs. Wilson, did
ample justice to the substantial fare set
before him, sustaining the while a three-
handed "crack" in the manner of a free,
hearty countryman of the world.

"What has come o' Margaret?" he
asked of Mrs. Wilson, during the last of
the three courses. "Tammas I hae seen
—Tammas is a chip o' the auld block,
Glen—that lad, Mrs. Wilson, wha leeves to
see't, wull no be a hair ahint his dad, and
that's no saying little, Glen. He's a steering chiel. Tammas kens what's what,
and that's what I like in young lads that
hae the warl' afore them. Agnes also I
hae seen, as comely and modest a lass as
e'er graced a farm-house, and as like
yoursel', Mrs. Wilson—at least what I fancy
you to hae been in the teens—as ony
dochter could be like her mither. But
Margaret—Margaret's the flower o' the

flock, Glen; there's nae doot aboot that—
Margaret I think mair o', Mrs. Wilson,
than a' the rest o' the family. I owe her a
debt that canna' weel be repaid. But
debts that canna' be repaid, Glen, should,
at the least, be acknowledg'd."

"Dootless! Ye're richt there, Tam!"
ejaculated the farmer.

"The hoose is unco fou o' folk jist noo,
as ye ken, Mr. Picardy," observed Mrs.
Wilson, "and we hae unco arrangements.
The sojers mess thegither at ae time, and
ithers follow. Margaret's attendin' to the
servants' denner in the kitchen enoo, but
I'm sure she'll hae nae objection to see ye
afore ye gang." And the farmer's wife
rose to clear away the table.

"But this trouble at the head of the
glen, Tam," said the farmer, drawing
nearer to his guest; "what pairt in't had
my dochter?"

"Pairt?" replied the drover in some confusion. "A' I ken is that she saved my life—a sma' saving it may hae been, but o' some consequence to me. Hay wad hae killed me, Glen, as dead as he wad hae killed Clavers the ither nicht, but Margaret stopped him—she did that—like a queen."

"Ay, ay! Dae ye say sae?" said the farmer, not a little perplexed by the *naïveté* of this declaration from Picardy, and unable to reconcile the circumstances in which such a clue of twofold murder could have arisen. "But hoo did Hay and ye encoonter?" said Glenvernoch; "I ken sae little aboot it. Werena ye maist to blame yersel, Tam? Tell the truth, man, and dinna fear the brood that comes oot o' an honest nest."

"I'll no say but I was rash, Glen, as ye wad probably hae been, stopped and worried to the throat on the road by an ootlaw nae better indeed than a highway robber. Gude kens, I'm nae better than my neebors. I pu'd my pistol—but had nae intent on the young man's life—aimed at his legs, and, missing him, he fell on me wi' his sword. In a second swordless Tam Picardy wad hae been carrion for the craws, but for the timely appearance and angry face o' your dochter Margaret."

"Weel, weel, Tam, we needna talk mair on that subject, an' the day rinning by," said the farmer. "Hoo mony nowt dae ye want?"

"A score at least," replied the drover.

"I'll bring ower a score and sax, sae he may hae some wale," observed Glenver-noch. "Sit and crack awee with the wife. I'll no be lang."

Mrs. Wilson, in her attentions to the drover, was coming and going, and had offered passing excuses for Margaret:

" We canna baith be wanted about the hoose at ae time."—" She's upstairs snoddin' hersel, but she'll be doon direckly" —when Margaret made her appearance.

She came into the parlour with a seam and a little workbox in her hands, and in the tidy dress of a farmer's daughter who has disposed of her main charge for the day, and means to devote herself to easier duties. But there was a steady application to her seam, after the first formal welcomes were over, which rather disturbed Picardy.

"I'm sae gled to see ye, mistress Margaret. Ye dinna ken hoo much I hae wished to see ye sin' the bruilzie up the glen. I may surely tak' this opportunity to thank you frae my heart."

"A pity," said Margaret, lifting her bright but lashed eyes a moment or two full on her visitor; " pity indeed, Mr. Picardy, that country folk canna meet

thegither wi' mair freedom and wi' less
suspicion, and should meet sae aften only
to brawl and fecht like enemies."

" Every word ye say is true as heeven,
mistress Margaret. Why shouldna kent
and honest folk meet in a' friendship and
say and dae what they please, no offensive
to their neebors. Here am I, Tam Picardy.
I mak' nae flesh o' ane or fish o' anither.
I wush to leeve and let leeve, and be freens
a' roon. And if it's the conventicles at the
Caldons ye are thinking o', mistress Margaret, nae power o' Government wad keep
me frae attending thae meetings as aften
as convenient. There's nae hairm in you,
or lady Martha, or ony ither lady, praying,
singing psalms, and hearing the Gospel
according to conscience. But there's a
neceesar distinction atween wurshippers
and armed rebels and caballers riding roon
the skirts o' the conventicle, and ready to

cut a' body's throats they hae an ill-will at."

"As lang as the services are conducted by ordained and godly men," replied Margaret, "decently and in order, as we hae a' heard and seen in the Kirk o' Scotland, what can be wrang wi' the wurshippers? I hae never seen ony sign o' rebelliousness. Are the folk to blame for being ready to defend themselves when they may be ridden ower and slain in cauld bluid by dragoons?"

"That's exactly what I aye say," rejoined the complacent but almost perplexed Picardy. "What the deil for no, as I should sweer, michtna the folk in the upper pairts here, far frae the parish kirk, no be allowed to hae their prayer meetings without being confoonded wi' the ootlaws and the wild fanatics? The Government's a stupid ass!" And Picardy, thinking he had now struck the right nail on the head, lifted his chair, and planted it down beside Margaret. "Tell me where lady Martha is, mistress Margaret—tell me, like a gude lass, ye maybe dinna ken whar she is—but let us a' tryst at the meeting, and I'll protect ye baith, on the richt hand and the left. I'll protect ye again' a' extremes."

Margaret, to whom this soft speech was nauseous as gall and wormwood, rose suddenly and seated herself with her seam at the end window of the parlour, leaving her work-box on the table.

"Baldoon himsel', indeed, has shared wi' me his anxiety to save lady Martha," continued Picardy, as if by a bold assertion to recover his lost ground.

"Dinna weave nets to your ain destruction, Tam," replied Margaret, with a calm but kindly look at the drover. "Thinkna ye that Sir David has ways and means o'

providing for lady Martha withoot as-
sistance from the like o' you? I wunner
tae hear ye aifter the warning ye had frae
Mister Hay."

"Hay, the ruffian! The maiden in the
Grass-market is the only bride he'll ever
kiss. I dinna care a spittle oot o' my
mooth for Hay, Margaret. Hae ye no
heard what the malignant has dune to
Clavers?"

"I hae heard," said Margaret, "but I
dinna believe ae-sided stories. Mr. Hay is
a young gentleman o' the country, lang
hunted and oppressed himsel', a' his family
trodden down on his account, no e'en his
old mother spared a cruel doom, as ye weel
ken, Tam. I'm sure if he should be driven
mad, the puir gallant lad, it wadna be
mickle speech."

"Hay will be d—d as sure as ye sit
there, Margaret Wilson!" exclaimed Pi-

cardy, clenching his teeth; and the young woman, shuddering, started to her feet, and glanced out of the window.

"I see the nowt coming owre the knowe," she said. "Ye'll hae to gang and attend to your business, Mr. Picardy. But remember what I have said," she added with a tone and look of authority, as she raised her forefinger, "Dinna follow or interfere wi' lady Martha; she'll no thank ye; and beware o' meeting Hay. There may be nane to staun atween you and him. Remember!"

With this admonition Margaret disappeared through the inner door of the parlour, leaving Picardy gaping after her in amaze and reverie. "Saucy proud lass that," he muttered; "naething bends her;" and then found his fingers twiddling the work-box, into which he looked, and there saw a ring which he had more than

once seen on the hand of Martha. He
picked it up, put it in his pocket, and
hastened out to meet Glenvernoch and the
cattle.

Nothing could be more agreeable in
country business than the bargaining of
the farmer and the drover on this occasion. Picardy was well pleased with the
beasts in their various points of breed,
bone, and flesh, and there remained only
the question of price, which the drover
left in the first instance to the farmer,
who named at once what he thought they
were fully worth. " Sic gran' nowt—no
the like o' them in the parish ; " at which
Tam shook his head, as if it would be hard
work to bring that money out of them " in
thae times." But as Glenvernoch and
Picardy returned to the parlour the
difference between them had been reduced
to small money.

"1 tell you what, Glen," said the drover, "I'll tak' the odd sax. Pit them to the score, and average the price a wee. There, noo, we are agreed, and here is the siller"—pulling out from under his belt a long purse of silver marks and gold nobles, from which the tale was soon told. "Keep the beasts in the infield, Glen, where the grass is green. I'll lift—na, let me see—I may be heavy enough handed coming doon—but I'll lift them within aucht days, a full week, that is, and a day or twa mair. Ha! ha! nae mair than that at the ootside, Glen."

And so saying, laughing and shaking hands with the farmer, Tam rode off, and in passing down to the gate had the honour of an almost military salute from Corporal M'Graw, to whom he had taken private occasion soon after his arrival to hand a military letter, of which he was the bearer, and in which the officer was enjoined to keep guard as agreeably to the family as might be, to let Margaret go where she pleased till further orders, but to watch her movements, keep note of her lengthened absences, and relax nothing of his vigilance as regarded all strangers coming on the farm.

# CHAPTER XIII.

It is the Sabbath-day: Creation sleeps
Cradled within the arms of heavenly love!
The mystic day, when from the vanquish'd grave
The world's Redeemer rose, and hail'd the light
Of God's forgiving smile.   Obscured and pale
Were then the plumes of prostrate seraphim,
Then hush'd the universe her sphere-born strain,
When from His throne, Paternal Deity
Declared the Saviour not in vain had shed
His martyr'd glory round the accursed Cross,
That fallen man might sit in Paradise,
And earth to heaven ascend in jubilee.

*Christopher North.*

ANOTHER Sabbath passed at Glenvernoch
without any movement on which the most
lynx-eyed inquisition could have fastened
the least suspicion of contumacy.   Mar-

garet had made no sign to either father or
mother of a desire to attend the Sunday
congregation at the Caldons. She loved
to go, would not willingly have been ab-
sent on any occasion, because it was the
desire, the necessary nourishment, and the
delight of her soul to join in those services
of public worship to which she had been
accustomed from her childhood, and
which exercised an extraordinary power
over her imagination, her faith, her visions
of the Eternal World, her whole spiritual
being. It was a devotion she owed to the
Supreme Object of Worship; it was
obedience to her Saviour and to His Word;
it was an essential employment of the
Sabbath-day, without which there could
be no keeping of the Fourth Command-
ment. All these were irresistible motives to
Margaret. That it was contrary to the
temporary law of the country to go did

not weigh against these considerations, in
her maiden simplicity and integrity of
heart, more than as dust in the balance.
That a wicked King, or wicked men seizing
on the Government in his name, should
have enacted such a law, was a profanity
to be struck with horror at, to be wept
over, but not a Baal to be bowed down to.
At the Caldons she had heard Presbyterian
ministers, who had remained faithful to
the doctrine and government of the Church
of Scotland, leading the devotion of the
people, and preaching the Gospel as they
had led and preached in the kirks from
which they were extruded. She had met
there people of like mind as herself, who,
without entering into any political leagues
or having any connexion with societies of
the time, streamed from the farm-houses
and shepherds' cots over many miles of
hill-country—north, south, east, and west

—to the place of worship. This was not only seemly to Margaret, but had the full approval and concurrence of her heart and conscience. It was like raising a tabernacle in the wilderness—grateful to God and inoffensive to man, even to kings and rulers—until the days of trial and wanderings should have passed away, when the Holy One, as she firmly believed, would revisit His beloved Zion with mercy, and build up anew its ruined walls.

Margaret, moreover, this Sabbath morning thought she would like to meet Martha. In the brief companionship of the young women ties of love and confidence had sprung up on both sides, rendered all the more binding by the congeniality of their religious principles, all the more penetrating by the differences of their character and circumstances. Margaret was touched by the romance and danger, the love and

the hatred, with which Martha was surrounded : Martha by the unexpected fervour, strength, and spirituality of resolution she had found in this high-minded
but artless maiden of the hills.   They had
recognized themselves as sisters able to
give and impart strength to each other.
Martha found in the purity and elevation
of Margaret's spirit  not only a sanction of
her own natural affections, but an *asbestos*
which they might much need in the cruci-
ble through which they were passing;
while her robust hold of life, her flows and
ebbs of worldly spirit—now soft and tear-
ful, sinking between devotion and despair,
now firm and defiant, rising on the threat-
ening billows—her easily recovered gaiety
of heart, and the merry laugh which would
ring from her sometimes in the darkest
hours, were as refreshing to the soul of
Margaret as showers and sunshine to a

spring flower bound in frost and snow,
and might be no less needful to her in a
world of which she had only recently begun to feel the rude impact. Much had
occurred in the brief interval since they
had separated. Yet no communication
had passed between them. How sweet a
few words with Martha, though only
snatched in the dismissal of the meeting !
Could Martha herself have any other desire?
Might she not be reproaching Margaret
for delaying attendance at the Caldons,
their only trysting-place ?

Margaret had seldom been more inclined to go to the conventicle, but the
knowledge that Picardy had proceeded
in the same direction threw a deep
shadow across her path. She dis-
trusted the drover, and the coarse
revelation he had made to her of a wild
passion, roused bodings of evil on a lower

range of life than she had hitherto expe-
rienced. There might be a disagreeable,
or, if Hay should happen to be present,
an appalling scene. The sensitive spirit
of the girl shrank from personal entangle-
ment in what might be a rude and violent
love affair, most of all on a scene where
every thought, feeling, and action should
be absorbed in divine worship. She had
missed the ring from her workbox, where
she usually kept it, loving to look at its
heavenly emblems, or to put it on her
finger in the evenings when at needle-
work. The loss had vexed her memory,
and though her suspicion had instantly
fallen on Picardy, yet she was unwilling
to let it rest there until she had made a
a more thorough search for the missing
token. But how could she meet Martha
and honestly conceal this burden on her
mind? Margaret was thus in a state of

irresolution, and a patient self-restraint from any step that might increase the freshly-bleeding anxieties of her parents, turned the scale in favour of staying at home.

And so it seemed that this family over whose life and destiny the harrows of oppression had begun to pass with ominous severity, could still enjoy in the solitude of their glen a day of Sabbath rest, with much of the calm solemnity, and peaceful joy and harmony, of the happier and more settled times. An air of cheerfulness, a reaction that was at least a contrast to previous gloom, brightened every countenance. Glenvernoch himself, looking round the land, could see little different from what had been. Grey clouds hung over much russet moorland, the light of the unseen sun only strong enough to bring into relief the greener patches round the farmhouse.

An inky mist blotted the fading colours of the woods of Cree, and the waters of the loch itself had a hue of lead long exposed to the weather. But with this atmospheric dulness in November the farmer was familiar. The scene would not have been home to him without it. If the finely-sloped but towering hills of Mony-gove had been swept away, or become volcanoes belching fire and smoke, he might have been disturbed in spirit. But there they stood, east and north, as self-contained and immovable as they had always stood—everlasting monitors to men to hold up their heads as long as they had heads on their shoulders—bright aerial splendours coursing along their summits fitfully, brighter one moment than the next, but palpable evidence that the sun was still shining in the heavens, and labouring through dense exhalations of cloud, and with all might of natural laws of ray-refraction, to be visible. Here was a token that God's world was not to be turned upside down by any mortal power. The farm and farmhouse, as well as the whole country round, seemed as if wrapped in Sabbatic stability and repose. The domestics and serving people, after much scrubbing and preparation on the Saturday eve, appeared as had been wont in new cleanliness of person and tidiness of dress on a day more wholly new and distinct than other days, all labour reduced to a minimum of necessity—with a common feeling not of idling or taverning, but of real jubilee of heart, uplifted to the Supreme Power over this troubled world. What a sweet breathing time amid all the vexations! Glenvernoch, as he saw and felt this, thanked God in the depths of his heart, and took courage.

Corporal M'Graw had marched down his men to the garrison-reading of prayers at Castle-Stewart, leaving two as sentries. The family and servants gathered round the upper end of the farm kitchen, where the mistress had laid the Old and New Testament. They came one by one, without formal request or pre-arrangement, spontaneously, instinctively—the servants bringing their stools with them and sitting down in the group, waiting as if it were a privilege, and happy in repossession of what had long been the sacred use and wont of the household. The farmer opened the worship, and a psalm having been sung, asked Margaret to read from " the Book." Margaret, in a clear but reverent and many-toned voice, read the 42nd chapter of Isaiah, and next the chapter of John's Gospel in which is given the divine conversation with the woman of

Samaria.   At the passage beginning,
"The hour cometh when neither in this
mountain nor yet at Jerusalem," &c., an
expression of heavenly joy passed over the
features of the reader.   It was as if some
new or deeper meaning had suddenly illuminated the mind and gladdened the heart
of the maiden—so instant, so unaffected,
so like a sunbeam was the light in her eyes
and on her face.   She paused and read the
passage a second time.   The hearers
caught more fully the significance of the
words, and with heartfelt response and
some share of her devotion and felicity of
spirit they followed Margaret in her short
prayer, concluding with, " Our Father."

One so shrewd and observant of worldly
details as Glenvernoch could not fail to
notice in course of the day that Picardy's
newly-bought herd, sated with better pasture than on the bleak moors, had mostly

lain down on the meadows, and were no exception to the general tranquillity round the farm house. But the drover himself was chewing his cud that afternoon in a different fashion. Picardy flattered himself that he was a legitimate, honourable and rising cattle dealer, and so in a sense he was; but in following the Government interest as much the most ready and lively support of his calling at the period, he had almost unconsciously ingrafted on his natural stock a slip of Government espionage, and to this sufficient complication he had further added an espionage of his own. He was a double spy, too ready to spy all round for authorities, themselves grossly unscrupulous, and a spy in particular over Martha and her relations to Hay, for the authorities in a secondary, for himself in a supreme sense. His fancy for Martha, long hidden in his heart as a hopeless dream, had warmed in proportion as his opportunity seemed supported by events, and like love-crazes, when combined with schemes of vulgar ambition, had grown hour by hour into a passion, not of the gentle, manly, or beautiful, but almost wholly of the leonine cast. Though he half believed he was following his business from principle, yet to trace Martha was the object that had really lured him on an expedition into a district where he had no allies, where there was no fellow-spy, and where to be suspected of being a spy might secure him an ignominious, if not still worse, reception. He knew all the hazard of it, but he had supplied himself with money, and by buying a few head of cattle here and there, and paying liberally in his jaunty way, he thought he would make friends, and learn something to the advantage of his own suit, and pleas-

ing to his chief patrons. His total failure
to make an unsuspecting ally of Margaret
was compensated by the happy accident
which had put him in possession of Martha's ring. This token in his hands would
be a mark of confidence from Margaret;
perhaps, if adroitly managed, from Sir
David of Baldoon himself.

Martha had taken up her abode, or rather
her devoted lover had chosen a retreat for
her, with military skill. The young lady
was not in any of the farm-houses, where
there is always more or less publicity, but
in a hut on the brow of one of those steep
mid-heights undistinguishable at a distance
from the mountain-side, but in reality one
of the hilly bastions looking down on much
world, with many a dreary gully and stiff
ascent behind to the mountain tops. No
cavalry could ride to it. Passengers on
foot, or mounted on the small shaggy hill-

ponies, alone could approach along a stiff and straggling track winding round the cliffy precipices, and forming a short road to the farm-house which stood at some distance, and with which the inmates of this humble dwelling were in intimate relation. It was inhabited by the mother-in-law of the farmer and an orphan grand-daughter. The hut, originally built against a natural escarpment of the mount, had been much improved by spade and shovel, as well as hammer and trowel, in the course of generations. A little garden slope had been made in front, and was fringed by the tops of mountain ashes springing in spindly height from lower declivities. Shrouded from view, it yet commanded an extensive prospect of country. The waters of Loch Trool shone like silver on a bright morning under the eye of any one looking out of the small casements, and at the southern ex-

tremity of the lake lay the woody dell of
the Caldons. It was somewhere on this
farm Picardy had surmised that lady
Martha was most probably to be found,
and for this reason he had sent forward his
attendant with a kindly premonition of
buying to the farmer, and with such hints
how the lad was to use his eyes until the
arrival of his master, as a cunning schemer
may give to an absolutely dependent
adept.

Martha had passed a week of much dis-
quietude. A rumour of Hay's attack on
Claverhouse in Newton of Glenken had
reached her remote eyrie in a tragic form,
exaggerated and distorted by every mouth
through which it had passed; and though
she had subsequently received a message
from Hay himself, giving a truer version,
and promising to be with her in a day or
two, yet so far he had not come. When in

her anxious watches she saw a grotesque
figure ascending the zig-zag towards the
hut, followed by or following, and sometimes
mounted on a rough four-footed animal
scarcely bigger than himself, and equally
grotesque, her alarm for the moment was
much increased. She associated him at
once with Picardy, and had no doubt that
the drover was near at hand. She feared
his discovery of her retreat; she feared
another encounter between him and Hay;
and in the flurry of her spirit, disturbed by
the previous excitement, imagined herself
lost in a web of crime and violence. She
ran into her apartment to hide her agitation, and was little more than in time to
conceal herself. The lad was in a few
minutes at the door of the hut, praying for
a drink of milk or even water.

" What brocht ye this gate, ye donnert
cratur. Gang your wa's to the farm-house

for milk, but if a drink o' water wull dae ye ony gude, there's a noggin' tae ye," said the mistress of the hut, as good as her offer.

The urchin drank, his eyes wandering eagerly over the stoup into the door and windows; and before leaving would fain have danced a somersault or two on the pony for the amusement of his hostess, but she drove him away.

The result of this incident was that Martha imparted to the farmer so vivid an impression of her own alarms, and of the danger that might arise to himself in allowing Picardy to come on the farm at so critical a juncture, that early next morning he anticipated the arrival of the drover, and helped by a neighbour with whom Tam had stayed overnight, kept him in such active exercise, looking at stock here and there, chaffering about prices, and yet

transacting nothing, that the baffled dealer
found himself driven for shelter late in the
afternoon to the house of the Caldons,
where it was necessary that he should be
wary as well as strictly orthodox in his
deportment. It was Saturday evening.
The preacher for the morrow had arrived,
and there was the usual preparation of an
evening meeting for prayer and catechism,
which all in the house had to attend, Picardy
among the rest, with a special examination
in his case as to his religious professions,
followed by admonitions as to the sin of
backsliding, the sin of Esau in selling his
birthright for a mess of pottage, the sin of
Sabbath-breaking, the unblessedness, yea
even the divine judgments, that were the
lot of worldly traffickers who laid not aside
their filthy lucre, their travellings, and their
pleasure-seekings on the Sabbath Day, to
bow in humble and reverent worship with

the chosen people, though it were only in the outmost courts of the Temple.

This severe penance was considerably softened to Picardy by the reflection that at the conventicle, having made his peace with the minister, he would have as sure and favourable an opportunity of seeing and accosting mistress Martha, of Baldoon, as any other. But in this expectation he was doomed to be disappointed. Martha did not appear. Margaret had stayed at home in a spirit of calm and self-restraining confidence, while Martha was detained by her disquiet, her sense of danger, and increasing anxieties as to the fate of Hay.

Chopfallen, fretful, and ill at ease with everything around him, Picardy set out from the Caldons under cover of night, rain falling and rivers swelling, along the Monygove side of the Cree; a dreary jour-

ney which tried his fortitude, but in course
of which he was still strong of heart enough
to meditate further and bolder strokes of
fortune.

## CHAPTER XIV.

Sweet as the smile when fond lovers meet,
And soft as their parting tear.

*Burns.*

MARTHA, on the following day, was walking
in the garden at noon, when the sun had
burst the barriers of cloud which had hung
dully over the sky all morning, and was now
shooting broad gleams of light through the
valleys, along the hills, and over the bosom
of the lake.    This day, she thought, would
bring her tidings of weal or woe.    The
Sunday meeting at the Caldons, besides its
more sacred character, was a centre of news.
So many came there from so many quarters

that some information of what had been passing in the outer world was sure to emerge on the Mondays. If not Hay himself, she would hear of Hay, truly or falsely, for good or for ill; and she longed to hear anything, whatever it might be. Her eyes had been anxiously directed along the steep path leading up past the hut, but no trace of any moving figure could be seen in that direction. The drover and his urchin had probably been disposed of for the present. Still more eagerly had she looked towards the southern end of the lake, whence boats sometimes issued to various points on the shore; to one near to the base of the rugged precipice over which she was standing. But no boat was visible. Shadows of a boat had seemed to appear and disappear more than once from her eyes, and she was standing in a dreamy fancy that she saw another when she became conscious of a footstep or a presence in the garden, and on turning round in half fright, there stood Hay, looking over her shoulders.

" Hay ! why surprise me so ? " she exclaimed, almost hysterically, as she dropped in her lover's arms.

Hay was booted and spurred, travel-stained, and bore all the marks of much recent haste and present fatigue.

" Martha, my dearest one," he said, " ever devoted Martha ! pardon me. I have not kept time. You will not think me here too soon, will you ? "

" Nay, nay," said Martha. " What was I saying ? " she asked, as she drew the fingers of both hands over her brow. " It was only a shock. O ! Willie ! how I have longed for you coming, and how glad now you are come ! "

" I should at least have taken half an hour to my toilet," said Hay.

" You are so sweet, so lovely, so like a
rose—"

" No more, pray ! " cried Martha, re-
covering her sunshine of smile and spirit.
" Roses are sweet indeed, but sometimes
tawdry enough in these wilds. If you had
been a minute longer I should have been
displeased, though you had been in the
brightest dress. But your toilet ! Well,
when I look, you are not the gay gallant I
have seen. These matted locks ; nay, here
are spots of mossy liquor on your cheeks ;
and these wearied eyes—ah ! my dear
Willie, you want more than toilet, you
want rest, perhaps even food. Come in !
come with me ! "

The lavatory and culinary resources of
the hut were brought to the service of Hay
with more than the usual warmth of hospitality, and when Martha and he sat down
together to a repast he felt refreshed both

in body and spirit; as hungry as a hawk, and as happy as a king. Martha was too willing to enjoy such rare moments of felicity to press any anxious conversation; her smiles tinkled into laughter, and she gave rein to her native humour, while her lover, in much the same mood, recounted jocularly various incidents since they had parted at the head of Glenvernoch. The " attempted assassination" of Clavers was told by Hay in graphic touches which for a moment alarmed, then amazed, and finally amused and satisfied his sweet-heart.

" You will stay with me now, Hay," said Martha, as they rose from the table. " What more can you do? You will stay, two, three, ever so many days here. You will not leave Glentrool for weeks—go no farther by day than you may return at night. What can you do now but wait

and look up to heaven for a help that
meantime is nowhere on earth?"

"Let us go out, Martha, before the
sun goes down," said Hay, looking out
of the casement, "and I will tell you
all."

They walked out, and wandered briefly
down untrodden parts of the precipice
where Martha had not ventured alone, but
the descent of which was rendered easy by
the firm foregoing step of Hay and his
ever ready hand—his arms to leap into, his
bosom to rest upon if need were—till they
came to a broad shelf, where the lake in its
circumference was spread out before them,
ahd the sound of its waters could be heard
laving the shore.

Hay glanced over the Loch, sun-rayed,
air-fanned, light and mobile, like some
more ethereal substance living and breathing, nay playing itself, in a wilderness of

dead material—his eyes resting chiefly on the dark woods of the Caldons.

" Tell me," said Martha.

" You would have me to abide here, love —in this little cup, yet a cup so full to overflowing of joy and sweetness "—said Hay, looking fondly into Martha's face—" a moment of this repays many weary hours. May it not be a foretaste of the larger life, the wider and more continuous scene, the sea, nay, as to this lake, the ocean of happiness before us ? "

" Do not speak in riddles, Hay—do not pray, be love-sick," urged Martha, though her eyes were melting in tenderness. " Tell me plainly."

" Martha, I have to go abroad," said Hay; " may never again see these scenes made dearer by their wildness and by our wildly mingled sufferings. Do not tremble so ! You will go with me, love. We shall never part. Light is breaking where we shall go, and whence we may soon return, it may be, to this very spot on some happy holiday of our lives. But there is one condition. I have vowed to rescue the good Dame, or die in the attempt."

"Your mother! Hay, ah! poor we!" exclaimed Martha. "How could we hope to live in fairest lands or under brightest suns with that heavy and accursed doom on one dearer to us than our own lives? Can it be done? How? Tell me and let us do it, God helping us."

"They cannot send the old lady to the plantations," replied Hay, "without carrying her over much Scotch ground. I can still assemble round me brave and trusty men on any line of march they choose. We shall attack the escort, and we shall triumph or—we shall fall."

"And I shall be with you," said Martha,

in a pensive, but firm and decided tone. " Put me in the muster-roll."

" Martha, Martha, what dost thou say? Art thou wise, or has thy sweet tongue run loose in despair? Such work is not a woman's."

" So many men are weaker than women that it becomes some women to be strong as men," said Martha, with the same collected and resolute air. " Give me a steed ! I'll put on a coat of mail, and case me round with pistols, each loaded to the primer with life and death. I shall follow thee over brae and fell, through flood and scaur, into the thick of war and slaughter, there kill and save to the last pistol, and be thy attending angel."

" I wonder at thee, true love, and yet why should I wonder ? " was the response of Hay. " Thy constancy has already passed through a furnace seven times heated. But still thy brave heart, yet a little while. All may be better ordered. I could tear my mother out of the tiger's claws any hour, but that is not enough. She must not only be rescued, but made safe and free. Kenmure, the weak but true and politic, is stirring in behalf of his kinswoman. If he succeed, the penalty would seem to be that I must bid a lasting adieu to Old Scotland."

"That is something," said Martha, uncomprehendingly, and clinging closer to her lover, as he looked eagerly towards the Caldons, already under shades of twilight, her eyes following the direction of his. "I surely see a boat on the loch," she said.

"Where?"

"In the sunbeam. It was there a moment since. There!"

"Ay, truly, love. It is Allan! my

faithful Allan! See how bravely he rows single-handed!" cried Hay, with enthusiasm, and forthwith gave a loud whistle, immediately answered by another equally loud from the boat.

"Come, Martha, come—he'll be on the strand before we get down!"

Allan delivered to his companion in arms and outlawry a missive, armorially sealed, which, in bold but not most legible characters, was as follows :—

"My friend and loveite,—These are to say that proposals have come to me from Wigtown to take Dame Hay, of Arioland, under watch and ward in this castle, whilk I am most willing to do for her sake, and yet find it against the grain to become a State jailor, with no hold over the issue. It is further hampered by the condition that a certain offensive person shall surrender himself to the laws, whilk is only,

indeed, killing the cub to save the dam, but
in whilk operation I cannot find free to be
a party.     Howsomever, the security of
the Dame is well worth having in hand,
and I shall see what can be compassed to
ordain that the offensive person aforesaid,
instead of being handcuffed to the maiden
in the Grassmarket, as he justly deserves,
shall depart the country under full cau-
tionary obligation and strict conditions
that he shall not bear arms against the
King, and sic ither.     Whether this will
succeed or no cannot meantime be said,
but think it your duty to make known,
advise, and warn the offensive person that
he must avoid all acts of war or violence,
and leave the matter, if it is to thrive, in
the hands for some time of, your servant,

" K."

Hay read aloud, as rapidly as he could

decipher, this important document, and seemed not unsatisfied with its contents. Martha was too well pleased with the general effect of the communication on her lover, and too kindly interested in Allan to trouble herself about any explanation of the somewhat dubious and caustic terms in which it was couched. She was meditating much hospitality to Allan as they toiled their way up to the hut; but to her entreaties that they should enter they were obviously too confident of their night's lodging elsewhere to listen, and on an assurance from Hay that he would see her next day, she allowed them to depart.

# CHAPTER XV.

The furtive fox crept in amang the corn,
And thocht he'd hae a glorious rise, man ;
But the Deil cam' fiddling through the toon,
And danced awa' wi' the exciseman.

*Medley.*

NEXT Sunday Picardy was again in the hill
country, pursuing cattle business, following
up transactions opened but not settled on
the former occasion, lifting stock really
his at Glenvernoch, and attending to the
various useful details of cattle-dealing life,
as he inwardly supposed to himself, and
convinced all outside parties by his talk of
bullocks, and his frank, jolly, and country-
like air.   Cattle-dealing had become so

brisk with the erst humble drover that he may almost be excused for thinking that the world, as it now went, revolved almost wholly on the sale, purchase, and other transfers of brute stock.

But this morning he had taken a position the most unlike, rather say the most grotesque for a gentleman cattle-dealer, now rising literally high in his profession. He had obviously no intention of doing worship at the conventicle. In horse and urchin, and pressure of business, he had kept miles away from the Caldons; but there he was, body and soul, that grey November matin, in not an undevout position one would say, for he was flat on the ground, with a natural screen of stone and fern before him that might be his crucifix or ornamental "reredos," but through which, in any case, he saw not unclearly every track to the Caldons on one side, and had a specially sweeping telescope of the long ascending zig-zag to Martha's hut. Indeed, he was lying there full length within a few paces' verge of the zig-zag, on one of its lower ascents, well armed, as usual, under his plaid doublet, and over him a camlet riding-cloak, as little distinguishable from the general russet as the fur of a hare in couch from that of a foumart gliding into its burrow. If found out, it might be taken for the last retreat of a " skulking Cove-nanter," with Clavers' dragoons in pursuit —a phantasmagoric figure, which Picardy would doubtless readily assume if need were.

No uncomfortable position that, even on a grey November morning, the hoar-frost melting under the heat of one's own large well-plaided body, like so much candy in the mouth of a baby. " A skulking Cove-nanter " had seldom the like of it. Well-

armed did we say ? Pistols, of course, and
here on the belt under the plaid-doublet a
sharp, short hanger, quite new, warranted
to cut a throat edgeways like a razor, or
pass through much fleshy and cartilaginous
substance in tierce and point-thrust—if
one should happen to be at short quarters
with a foe. But had Picardy no other arms
than these in his open character as cattle-
dealer, and visibly rising man, in leonine
though invisible love of a well-born but
distressed damsel, whom to rescue and
make one's own for life would surely be
a stroke of fortune? Had he not the
ring purloined from Margaret's workbox,
Martha's precious pledge, and had he not
been at Baldoon, cattle-dealing, and there,
with diplomacy, audacity, and cool insinu-
ating deception as of the devil, advancing
step by step into good graces with the
Laird, produced the ring as certificate of

confidentiality, till the old Baron, all too agitated and broken those some days past by tragic rumours of Hay and the too certain misery of his daughter, shook with agony, wept, and stormed in his dotage.

"Neither tale nor talesman, Tam! Anither o' the mysteries!" said the Baron, glancing with contemptuous ruefulness at Picardy as he thought of possible treachery. "Art sure, man, thou hast not stown the ring?"

"It comes from one who is gude freen wi' lady Martha, and whom lady Martha is gude freen wi'," replied Picardy, in un-abashed assurance. "It returns from me to your daughter, innocent young lady, whom I wad gladly befreend."

And though Picardy failed of his pur-pose, which was no less than to obtain some message or commission from Sir David that would not only commend his

visits to Martha, but might in certain circumstances be a cover for her forcible
abduction, yet he so far prevailed that the
wary but perplexed Baron took his pen,
and writing his name with his seal under
it, said, " Nae loose writings, and nae loose
words on loose tongues, but if ye can be
trusted ow'r the doorstep, and no a mere
tell-tale traitorous pyet, there's as gude as
ye hae brocht, Tam, and I'll see gif ye're
an honest man. As for the stots and
heifers, that's a matter o' less consequence.
We're agreed."

With this autograph in his breast-pocket,
and otherwise well armed, the drover lay
on his watch that Sabbath morning not
uncomfortably. The day seemed big with
destiny. At the least, his quiet and
prostrate position, seeing most things while
unseen, and ready to become " skulking
Covenanter " at any moment if necessary,

was safe, and should surely reveal something more or less notable, useful.

And now when the lazy November sun
is at length making some progress, filling
the hollows with irradiated mist, striking
more countless millions of glittering dia-
monds from every hanging and falling leaf,
from blades of grass and waving ferns,
from the warm surface of the vitreous
granite rocks, and from the frosty bosom
of their brown lichens, with intervening
spaces of pink and blue spreading from a
central fire in the sky, muffled in upper
vapours through which the solar bright-
ness seems advancing from afar in glorious
triumph, and the whole scene is thus
invested with a rude but mystical and gor-
geous splendour beyond the conception of
a Picardy, other objects more distinctly
visible to our devotional friend begin to
appear in quick succession.    Human

figures are seen moving along various
tracks, down every hill-side, and along the
margins of the lake. They appear in the
distance like dwarfs, but they are moving,
and they come nearer and bigger, some in
Indian file, some in groups, and some way-
worn and fierce-like stragglers taking
short-cuts across the moory land, but all
converging to a common centre. Those
who come first appear, from their flushed
faces and loose hair, to have travelled far-
thest, most on foot, a few on rough ponies,
all attended by sheep-dogs, and armed at
least with thundering sticks. After these
what seem families, in more composure—
husbands and wives, with boys and girls,
and old men tottering on their staffs.
Much this latter order of procession has
passed down the zig-zag where Picardy's
attention, there in his screened and hori-
zontal rest, has been chiefly directed—

when lo! is it possible? Here comes
surely Martha, bright as the morning;
alone; a young girl only, with a Bible in
her hand, at her side; in charming grace
and freedom of attire, her cloak and hood
over her arm.    Good heaven! it is she,
even she!  Queen of the May, one must
look at you if at nothing else!  And the
gloating eyes of Picardy followed Martha long after the rustle of her silk, as she
stepped onward a few paces from his hiding place, had passed away; and when he
looked round from his reverie, the last of
the moving figures had disappeared in the
defiles and woody shades of the Caldons.

Picardy had now a solitary interval,
where we must leave him for a little, forti-
fied by the flask of usquebaugh and the
snaps with which he had providently fur-
nished himself.  His thoughts and sensa-
tions were wholly of a pleasant character.

Through overhanging trees of oak and silver birch the conventicle has disappeared
from all spying eyes—disappeared almost
to itself for a time, so various and narrow
are the tracks by which they advance under
cover of this natural forest, in some parts
dense, in others sparse, and moving with
light and shadow.   At length they gather
in an open space, where there is a firm
green sward, and the sun shines with the
whole light of day.   On one side of the
glade is a dwelling-house nestled amid old
trees, the larger of the forest, under which
in cold or stormy weather divine worship
can proceed with tolerable comfort to de-
vout souls.   But there is a little mound in
the open space, and a table and arm-chair
have been set down upon it this morning,
the day is so fine; solar heat distinctly per-
ceptible.   The first comers and the men on
ponies have gathered about the house,

coming out and going in. But others have
taken their places in front and on the sides
of the little mound. Martha has sat down
on a seat which seems prepared for her
near one end of the table, and a younger
woman, a girl in form, but reverent and
saint-like beyond her years, walks round
from the other side, to whom Martha rises,
holds out her hand with a surprised but
rapturous smile, and kisses most sisterly.
A new stream of worshippers issues from
the dwelling-house, and after them comes
the minister of the day, by himself—in the
prime of early manhood, spare in person but
of intellectual countenance, and eyes glow-
ing with fires of enthusiasm, repressed,
under control, almost latent this morning,
one would say, under a mild celestial light of
pure and humble devotion. It is Renwick!
In some disfavour with the moderate Pres-
byterians, his favour for the Covenant

placing him almost on a line with Richard Cameron; and though for some while "marked for judgment" in the Grassmarket, yet at his peril has come into Galloway, now completely under the heel of Claverhouse as believed, on a mission of reconciliation—to heal divisions, and to beseech men in the name of God to be patient, and to suffer valiantly but wisely. The eyes of all are directed to the minister as he approaches the table, curious to observe one of whom many have heard but few have seen before. He leads the divine service of the Scotch Church, himself joining and mingling strong chords of bass in the psalmody; reads a chapter from the Scriptures; offers prayer in what may be called breathings of the soul, for the sentences are short and solemn, as if drawn from the depths of the heart; and then preaches from a sacred text, dwelling on

the unity of the Christian people, denounc-
ing all self-will and will-worship, and as to
the persecutions, scornfully asks what are
they in comparison with the Truth of God,
or with the Sufferings of the Redeemer,
but light afflictions of the moment which
work out a more exceeding and eternal
weight of glory. The sermon is followed
by prayer, psalmody, and benediction; and
the conventicle, deeply impressed, scatters
and betakes itself home.

Picardy—who had watched eagerly the
gathering of this assembly, new, visionary,
and almost like a dream to him—had to
watch as eagerly for its dispersion. The
time seemed to him long—nearly three
hours; but his course was simple. Martha would return by the way she had gone;
he would follow her as an attender of the
conventicle, and use all the potions of
which he was possessed in a frank, friendly,

genial spirit.  A foundation would be laid
if not of the true love-artist type, of solid
brick-and-mortar masonry, on which a
sweet and towering superstructure might
perchance arise, when it should be all over
with Hay, and an imaginative crisis should
have come.

The order of procession was reversed on
the return.  It was the groups, the families, that came first.  Again the lovely face,
the developed bust, the light step, the
fearless and mirthful air of Martha, but
with her?  Oh, horror to my waxy eye-
balls?  Whose is that tall and slender
figure, that pale, serious face, those long-
lashed eyes bent towards the ground, with
Martha?  They have taken the little girl
between them, and given her each a hand
as they ascend.  The child is almost leap-
ing with joy, looking up to one face and
the other,  putting questions,  receiving

answers. One can hear the voices now as they pass.

" Not a sparrow falls to the ground without the will of the Father," said Martha.

" Sparrows flee away from the bad men," said the little orphan.

" And Christ carries His lambs in His bosom, my dear," was the voice of the tall figure.

" Curse that Margaret of Glenvernoch !" growled Picardy from the bottom of his stomach, as he rolled behind his altar-screen of stone and fern, and saw all his devices founded on the ring falling like a house of cards into a useless heap. He clutched the withered herbs around him in his anger, and rolled again from side to side in his disappointment. Ha ! a convulsive start ! What do the waxy eye-balls now see that they are so transfixed, and the whole body of Picardy has now got upon its fours ?

Almost incredible to Picardy in his present desolation ! Hay himself, by jeopardy, passing along a divergent track, the Minister leaning on his arm ; his rapier at his side, not dangling, but firmly reposing along that well-shaped limb ; unseen at this distance indeed, save its brightly-mounted hilt, from which the sun's rays, now and again, elicit blinding sparks as of lightning.   How free, noble, and  strong he walks !   And those stalwart men before and behind ! Gadamercy, of what avail are two pistols and a short hanger here ! The sooner the sun sets and one can scamper out of this dog-hole the safer for one's skin, however tough.

END OF VOL. II.

GILBERT AND RIVINGTON, PRINTERS, ST. JOHN'S SQUARE, LONDON.

www.ingramcontent.com/pod-product-compliance
Lightning Source LLC
Chambersburg PA
CBHW030800020726
47499CB00006B/1710